FIVE GO TO DEMON'S ROCKS

FIVE GO TO DEMON'S ROCKS

ENID BLYTON

Illustrated by
Eileen A. Soper

Hodder
Children's
Books

a division of Hodder Headline plc

First published in Great Britain in 1961
by Hodder and Stoughton

This edition 1997

10 9 8 7 6 5 4 3 2

A catalogue record for this book is available from the
British Library

ISBN 0 340 71491 3

Typeset by Hewer Text Composition Services, Edinburgh
Printed and bound in Great Britain by
Clays Ltd, St Ives plc

Hodder Children's Books
a division of Hodder Headline plc
338 Euston Road
London NW1 3BH

CONTENTS

CHAPTER ONE

Three visitors arrive

'FANNY!' SHOUTED Uncle Quentin, running up the stairs with a letter in his hand. 'FANNY! Where are you?'

'Here, dear, here, helping Joanna with the dusting,' said Aunt Fanny, appearing out of a bedroom. 'Don't shout like that. I'm not deaf, you know. What's the matter?'

'I've a letter here from that old friend of mine, Professor Hayling,' said Uncle Quentin. 'You remember him, don't you?'

'Do you mean the man who came here to stay a few years ago, and kept forgetting to come in for meals?' said Aunt Fanny, flicking some dust off her husband's coat.

'Fanny, don't flick at me like that,' said Uncle Quentin crossly. 'Anyone would think I was covered in dust. Listen – he's coming to stay *today* for a week – instead of next week.'

Aunt Fanny stared at her husband in horror. 'But he *can't* do that!' she said. 'George is coming home today – and her three cousins with her, to stay. You know that!'

'Oh – I'd forgotten,' said Uncle Quentin. 'Well, ring up and tell George to stay where she is – we can't have them while Professor Hayling is here. I shall want to be quite undisturbed – he and I have to confer about some new

1

invention of his. Don't look like that, my dear – this may be very, very important.'

'Well, it's important to the Five that *their* plans shouldn't be spoilt,' said Aunt Fanny. 'After all, George only went to stay with Dick, Julian and Anne because you had some urgent papers to write, and you didn't want to be disturbed – and you *knew* today was the day they were due home. Quentin, you must ring up your professor friend and say he can't come.'

'Very well, my dear, very well,' said Uncle Quentin. 'But he won't like it. He won't like it at all!' He went off to his study to use the telephone, and Aunt Fanny hurried up the stairs to get ready the rooms for the four cousins.

'Anne can sleep with George as usual,' she said to Joanna. 'And the two boys can sleep in the guest room.'

'It will be nice to have all the Five back again,' said Joanna, pushing the vacuum cleaner up and down the landing. 'I miss them – and you should see the cakes I made yesterday – two whole tins full!'

'You're too good to those children, Joanna,' said Aunt Fanny. 'No wonder they're so fond of you. Now, we'll – oh dear – there's my husband calling me again. All right, dear, I'm coming, I'm coming!'

She ran downstairs to the hall, and into the study. Uncle Quentin was standing there, holding the telephone receiver. 'What shall I do?' he almost shouted. 'Professor Hayling has left and is already on his way here. I can't stop him coming. And he's bringing his son with him, so there are two of them.'

'His *son*! Well, really!' said Aunt Fanny. 'There isn't room for them here, with the four cousins as well, Quentin. You know that.'

'Well, ring up George and tell *her* not to come back for a week, but to stay with her cousins,' said Uncle Quentin, crossly. 'There's no reason why they should ALL come here.'

'But, Quentin, you *know* perfectly well that George's aunt and uncle are shutting up the house today, and going on a cruise somewhere,' said Aunt Fanny. 'Oh dear, oh dear! Well, I'll ring up George, and try to stop them all coming!'

So once more the telephone was used, and Aunt Fanny tried anxiously to get in touch with George. For a long time nobody answered, and then at last a voice came. 'Hallo – who's there?'

'Mrs Kirrin here – may I speak to George, please?'

'Oh – I'm sorry – they've already left, on their bicycles,' said the voice. 'And the house is empty except for me. I'm a neighbour come in to lock everything up. I'm so sorry I can't get George for you.'

'Oh – thank you. Never mind!' said Aunt Fanny, and put back the receiver. She gave a heavy sigh. NOW what was to be done? Professor Hayling and his son were on their way to Kirrin Cottage – and so were the Five – and none of them could be stopped. What a household it would be!

'Quentin,' she said, going into the study where her husband was tidying up enormous piles of papers. 'Quentin, listen – George and all the others are on their way here. And HOW I am going to put everyone up, I do not know. It looks as if somebody will have to sleep in Timmy's kennel, and I've a good mind to make a bed up for *you* in the coal-house!'

'I'm busy,' said Uncle Quentin, hardly listening. 'I've all these papers to get in order before Professor Hayling comes. And by the way, my dear, will you PLEASE tell the children to be quiet while the professor is here – he's rather short-tempered, and . . .'

THREE VISITORS ARRIVE

'Quentin, *I'm* beginning to feel rather short-tempered too,' said Aunt Fanny. 'And if . . .' She stopped very suddenly and gazed through the study window in horror. Then she pointed her finger at it. 'Look! What's that at the window?'

Her husband turned and stared in amazement. 'It looks like a *monkey*!' he said. 'Where on earth did it come from?'

A voice called down the stairs. It was Joanna. 'There's a car at the door – I think it's your visitors – a man and a boy!'

Aunt Fanny was still staring in astonishment at the monkey, who was now scratching at the window-pane, chattering in a funny little prattle. He pressed his nose to the glass, just like a child.

'DON'T tell me that your friend owns a monkey – and has brought *him* to stay too!' groaned poor Aunt Fanny. She jumped as a loud bang came from the front door, and went to open it.

Yes – there stood Professor Hayling, the man who had so often forgotten to come in for meals when he had stayed at Kirrin Cottage years before. And by him was a boy of about nine, with a face a little like that of the monkey now on his shoulder!

The professor strode in, calling to the taxi driver behind. 'Bring the luggage in please. Hallo, Mrs Kirrin – nice to see you again. Where's your husband? My word, I've some interesting news to tell him. Ah, Quentin, there you are! Got your papers all ready for me?'

'My dear old friend!' said Uncle Quentin, shaking hands warmly. 'Fine to see you! So glad you could come.'

'This is Tinker, my son,' said Professor Hayling, clapping the boy on the back, and almost knocking him over. 'I always forget what his real name is – we call him Tinker because he's always tinkering with cars – mad on them, you know! Shake hands, Tinker. Where's Mischief?'

Poor Aunt Fanny hadn't been able to get in a word. The professor was now in the hall, still talking. The monkey leapt off the boy's shoulder, and was on the hallstand, swinging on a hat-peg.

Really, it's like a circus! thought poor Aunt Fanny. And the rooms not prepared yet – and what about lunch? Oh my goodness – and all the cousins coming as well. What *is* that monkey doing now? Making faces at himself in the hall mirror!

Somehow or other the visitors were pushed into the living room, and they sat down. Uncle Quentin was so anxious to discuss some mighty problems with the professor that he actually fetched a great sheaf of papers and immediately spread them over the table.

'*Not* in here, dear – in your study please,' said Aunt Fanny, firmly. 'Joanna! Will you help me take the bags up to the guest room? And we can make up a bed there on the couch for the little boy. There won't be room anywhere else.'

'What about the monkey!' asked Joanna, eyeing it warily. 'Is he to have a bed too?'

'He sleeps with me,' said Tinker, in an astonishingly loud voice, and suddenly leapt up the stairs, making a most extraordinary purring noise as he went. Mrs Kirrin stared after him in amazement.

'Is he in pain, or something?' she said.

'No, no – he's just being a car,' said his father. 'I told you he was mad about cars. He can't help pretending to be one now and again.'

'I'm a car, a Jaguar car!' yelled Tinker, from the top of the stairs. 'Can't you hear my engine! R-R-R-R-R-R-R! Hey, Mischief come and have a ride!'

The little monkey scampered up the stairs and leapt on to the boy's shoulder, chattering in its funny little voice. The Jaguar car then apparently made a tour of all the bedrooms, occasionally giving a very loud honk.

'Does your boy always behave like that?' asked Uncle Quentin, amazed. 'How do you manage to do any work?'

'Oh, I have a soundproof workroom in my garden,' said the professor. 'I hope your workroom is sound-proof, too?'

'No, it isn't,' said poor Uncle Quentin, still hearing the 'car' upstairs. What a boy! How could anyone bear him for more than two minutes? And to think he had come to STAY!

He shut the study door after the professor – but no door could shut out the sound of the small boy honking upstairs!

Poor Aunt Fanny was eyeing all the luggage brought in. Why hadn't the professor gone to a hotel? What was life going to be like, with the Five here, and the professor, and a small boy who apparently thought he was some kind of car all the time. To say nothing of a monkey called Mischief! And WHERE were they all going to sleep?

CHAPTER TWO

A little excitement

GEORGE AND her three cousins were already on their way back to Kirrin. They cycled along the lanes with Timmy, George's dog, loping easily beside them.

'Won't it be fun to be at Kirrin Cottage again!' said Anne. 'It's so lovely to look out of a window and see Kirrin Bay, blue as the sky! I vote we go over to the Island for a picnic!'

'You'll like to have your own kennel again, won't you, Timmy?' said George, and Timmy gave her ankle a quick lick, and barked.

'It's always so peaceful at Kirrin Cottage,' said Dick. 'And your mother's so kind and jolly, George. I hope we shan't upset Uncle Quentin with our talk and fun.'

'I don't *think* Father has any very important work on hand,' said George. 'Anyway, he'll only have you for a week – it's a pity that professor friend of his is coming in a week's time, or you could have stayed longer.'

'Well, a week is quite a nice long time,' said Julian. 'Hallo – there's our first glimpse of Kirrin Bay, look – as blue as ever!'

They were all glad to see the little blue bay, and to catch sight of Kirrin Island lying there peacefully in the sun.

A LITTLE EXCITEMENT

'You're lucky, George, to have an island all of your own,' said Anne. 'One that is really and truly yours!'

'Yes, I *am* lucky!' said George. 'I was never so pleased in all my life as the day Mother gave it to me. It's belonged to our family for years, of course – and now it's mine! We'll go over there tomorrow!'

At last they came to the end of their journey. 'I can see the chimneys of Kirrin Cottage!' said Julian, standing up on the pedals of his bicycle. 'And the kitchen fire is going – I can see smoke. I hope dinner's cooking!'

'I can smell it!' said Dick, sniffing. 'I think it's sausages.'

'Idiot!' said the other three together, and laughed. They rode up to the back gate, and leapt off their bicycles. They put them into the shed, and George gave a shout!

'Mother! We're *home*! Where are you?'

She had hardly finished yelling when Anne suddenly clutched her arm.

'George – what's that? Look! Peeping out of the window there!'

They all looked – and George shouted in astonishment: 'It's a monkey! A MONKEY! No, Timmy. No – come back! TIMMY!'

But Timmy too had seen the quaint little face peering out of the window, and had shot off to investigate. Was it a small dog? Or a strange sort of cat? Anyway, whatever it was, he was going to chase it away! He barked at the top of his voice as he galloped indoors, and almost knocked over a small boy there. The monkey, terrified, at once leapt on to the picture-rail than ran round the room.

A LITTLE EXCITEMENT

'You leave my monkey alone, you big bully you!' cried a furious voice; and through the open door George saw a small boy give Timmy a sharp smack. She raced indoors, and gave the small boy a smack as sharp as the one he had given Timmy! Then she glared at him angrily.

'What are you doing here? How DARE you hit my dog? It's a good thing he didn't eat you up. And what's that creature doing up there?'

The little monkey was terrified. It sat clinging to the picture-rail, trembling, making a piteous chattering noise. Julian came in just as Joanna arrived from upstairs.

'What's all this?' she said. 'You'll have your father racing out of his study in a minute, George. Stop barking at the little monkey, Timmy, for goodness' sake! And stop crying, Tinker, and take your monkey away before Timmy eats him.'

'I'm NOT crying,' said Tinker fiercely, rubbing his eyes. 'Come here, Mischief. I won't let that dog hurt you! I'll – I'll . . .'

'You take your monkey away,' said Julian gently, thinking that the small boy was very brave to imagine he could fight old Timmy. 'Run along.'

Tinker made a clicking sound and the monkey dropped at once on to his shoulder, and nuzzled there. It put its tiny arms round the boy's neck, and made a little choking noise.

'Oh – poor little mite – it's crying!' said Anne. 'I didn't know monkeys could cry. Timmy, don't frighten it again,

11

please don't. You mustn't bully tiny things.'

'Timmy never bullies anything!' said George at once, frowning at Anne. 'But after all, what do you expect him to do when he comes home and finds a strange boy *and* a monkey here. Who are you, boy?'

'I shan't tell you,' said Tinker, and marched out of the room, the monkey still whimpering into his neck.

'Joanna – who on earth is he?' asked Dick. 'And what is he doing here?'

'I thought you wouldn't like it,' said Joanna. 'It's that professor friend of your father's, George – the one who was coming to stay next week. He telephoned this morning to say he was coming *this* week instead – and bringing his boy as well! He didn't say anything about a monkey, though!'

'Are they *staying* here?' said George, in horror. 'How *can* Mother let them – she *knew* we were all coming today! How *mean* of her, how . . .'

'Be quiet, George,' said Julian. 'Let Joanna go on.'

'Well, they arrived before anything could be done to stop them,' said Joanna. 'And now your father is shut up in his study with Professor Hayling – the boy's father – and your mother and I are at our wits' end to know where to put you all. The boy and his father – and I suppose the monkey too – are sharing the guest room.'

'But that's where Julian and Dick were going to sleep!' said George, losing her temper again. 'I'll go and tell Mother that boy can't stay, I'll . . .'

'Don't be silly, George,' said Julian. 'We'll manage somehow. We can't go back home because our house will be all shut up now.'

'You could sleep up in the loft,' said Joanna, sounding rather doubtful. 'But it's very dusty and terribly draughty. I could put a couple of mattresses up there for you.'

'All right,' said Julian. 'We'll make do up in the loft. Thanks, Joanna. Where's Aunt Fanny? Does she mind all this?'

'Well – she's a bit rushed,' said Joanna. 'But you know what your aunt is – always so kind, never thinks of herself. That Professor Hayling! Just walked into the house as if he owned it, bringing luggage and that most peculiar little boy – and a *monkey*! Though the monkey seems a nice enough little thing. It came and watched me wash up, and bless me if it didn't try to dry the plates for me!'

The kitchen door swung open and George's mother came in. 'Hallo, dears!' she said smiling. 'I thought I heard Timmy barking. Dear Timmy – wait till you see the monkey!'

'He's seen him already,' said George, scowling. 'Mother, how *could* you take people in when you knew we were coming home today?'

'That's enough, George,' said Julian, who saw how worried his aunt looked. 'Aunt Fanny, we won't be ANY trouble! We'll keep out of the house as much as we can, we'll do the shopping for you, we'll go across to Kirrin Island and keep out of your way, we'll . . .'

13

'You're kind, Julian,' said his aunt, and smiled at him. 'Things *will* be rather difficult – especially as Professor Hayling never can remember to come to meals on time, and you know what your uncle is! He could forget breakfast, dinner and supper for a whole year, and then wonder why he felt hungry!'

That made everyone laugh. Julian slipped his arm round his aunt and gave her a hug. 'We'll sleep in the loft,' he said, 'and enjoy it, too. We will help with the housework and we'll do any odd jobs too. You've no idea how fine I look with an apron round my waist, and a broom in my hand!'

Even George smiled at the idea of Julian wearing an apron. Then Timmy went suddenly to the half-open door and barked. He could smell that monkey again. He heard a high chattering noise, and pushed the door open at once. What! Was that monkey calling him rude names?

He saw the little creature sitting on the top of the rail at the foot of the stairs. It saw Timmy, and danced up and down, sounding as if it were laughing. Timmy raced to the rail and leapt up, barking fiercely.

The study door flew open and out marched not one angry professor, but two!

'WHAT'S ALL THIS NOISE? CAN'T WE HAVE A MOMENT'S PEACE?'

'Oh *dear*!' said Aunt Fanny, foreseeing this kind of thing happening twenty times a day, now that Timmy and the others were here. She shushed the two angry men.

A LITTLE EXCITEMENT

'Now, now – Timmy just isn't used to the monkey yet. Go back, please, and shut the door. I'll see you aren't disturbed again!'

'WOOF-WOOF!' shouted Timmy, using his very loudest bark, and Professor Hayling shot back into the study at top speed!

'Any more rudeness from Timmy and I'll have him sent away!' roared Uncle Quentin, and he too disappeared.

'WELL!' said George, her face red with anger. 'What does he mean by *that*, Mother? If Timmy goes, I go too! Oh, *look* at that monkey – he's sitting on top of the grandfather clock now! *He* ought to be sent away, horrid little mischievous thing – not old Timmy!'

CHAPTER THREE

Mischief, Tinker – and Timmy!

JULIAN AND Dick set to work to take a couple of old mattresses up to the loft, and some rugs and a couple of cushions for pillows. It *was* rather draughty! But what else was to be done? It was still too cold to sleep outside in a tent.

George was very sulky. 'That scowl will *grow* on your face, George, if you aren't careful,' said Dick. 'Cheer up, for goodness' sake. It's worse for your mother than it is for any of us. She's going to be very busy this week.'

She certainly was! Meals for nine people, five of them very hungry children, were not easy to provide. Joanna did an enormous amount of cooking, the four children helped with the housework and cycled off to Kirrin village in the mornings to do the shopping.

'Why can't that boy Tinker help?' demanded George, on the second day they were at home. 'What on earth does he think he's doing now? Look at him out in the garden rushing all round, making a frightful noise. Tinker, shut up! You'll disturb your father and mine.'

'You shut up yourself!' called back Tinker, rudely. 'Can't you see I'm a Mercedes car, with a very powerful engine? And see how well it stops when I put on the brakes – no jerk at all! And hear the horn – marvellous!'

16

He gave a remarkably good imitation of a powerful car horn. At once the study window shot up and two very angry men shouted together:

'TINKER! What do you think you're doing, making that noise? You've been told to be QUIET!'

Tinker began to explain about the Mercedes, but as this didn't seem to satisfy either of the angry men, he offered to be a little Mini. 'You see, it goes like this,' said Tinker, beginning to move off, making a low purring noise, 'and it . . .'

But the window was slammed shut, so the little Mini drove itself into the kitchen, and said it was very hungry, could it have a bun?

'I don't feed cars,' said Joanna. 'I have no petrol. Go away.'

The Mini purred out of the kitchen on its two legs, and went to look for passengers. Mischief the monkey scampered up, and ran up Tinker's body to his shoulder.

'You're my passenger,' said Tinker, and Mischief held on to his hair as he drove all round the garden at top speed, honking every now and again, but very quietly indeed.

'He's a funny child,' said Joanna to Mrs Kirrin, when she came into the kitchen. 'Not bad really – him and his cars! I've never seen a child so mad on them in my life! One of these days he'll turn into one!'

It began to rain next day and Tinker couldn't go out. He nearly drove everyone mad, rushing about all over the house hooting, and purring like a car engine.

'Now look,' Joanna said to him, when, for the twentieth time, he drove himself all round her kitchen. 'I don't care if you're a Mini, or a Ford Fiesta, or even a Rolls – you just keep out of my kitchen! It's a funny thing to think that a fine car like a Rolls can steal a bun out of my tin – it ought to be ashamed of itself!'

'Well, if I can't get petrol, I've got to get *something* to run on, haven't I?' demanded Tinker. 'Look at Mischief – *he's* helping himself to apples in the larder, but you don't say anything to him!'

'Oh, lands sakes, is that creature in the larder again?' cried poor Joanna, rushing across the kitchen. 'Who left it open, I'd like to know?'

'Timmy did,' said Tinker.

'You little liar!' said Joanna as she shooed Mischief out

of the larder. 'Timmy would never do a thing like that. He's as honest as the day, not like that little thief of a monkey of yours!'

'Don't you like him?' said Tinker, sorrowfully. 'He likes *you*.'

Joanna glanced across at the tiny monkey. He sat huddled in a corner, his arms over his face, looking very small and sad. One small brown eye peeped out at Joanna.

'You're a humbug, you are!' said Joanna. 'Looking as if you're the unhappiest monkey in the world, when all the time you're thinking what mischief to do next. Here – come and get this biscuit, you rascal – and don't you dare to go near Timmy this morning. He's very very angry with you.'

'What did Mischief do to Timmy?' asked Tinker, surprised.

'He went to Timmy's dish and stole one of the bones there,' said Joanna. 'Timmy growled like a roll of thunder! I really thought he would bite off the monkey's tail. My word, you should have seen Mischief skedaddle!'

Mischief had now crept up cautiously to Joanna, eyeing the biscuit she held. He had had one or two slaps from her for stealing, and he was rather wary of her quick right hand.

'Here you are – take the biscuit, for goodness' sake,' said Joanna. 'And don't look such a little misery, or I might suddenly find myself giving you another biscuit. Hallo – where's he gone?'

The monkey had snatched the biscuit with one of his tiny paws, and had scampered away to the door. It was shut, so Tinker opened it for him. At once Timmy came in. He had been lying outside the door, sniffing the good smell of soup cooking on the stove.

Mischief leapt to the top of a chair back and made a strange little whinnying sound – rather apologetic and sad. Timmy stood still and pricked up his ears. He understood animal language very well!

Mischief still held the biscuit. He leapt down to the seat of the chair – and then, to Joanna's enormous surprise, he held out the biscuit to Timmy! He chattered in a very small voice, and Timmy listened gravely. Then the big dog took the biscuit gently, threw it into the air, chewed it once, and swallowed it!

'Well, did you ever see anything like *that* before!' said Joanna, marvelling. 'For all the world as if Mischief was apologising to Timmy for stealing his bone – and offering him his biscuit to make up! Well, whatever will George say when she hears!'

Timmy licked his lips to see if any biscuit crumbs were left, and then put his big head forward, and gave the monkey a sudden lick on the tip of his funny little nose.

'Timmy's saying thank you!' cried Tinker, in delight. 'Now they'll be friends – you see if they won't!'

Joanna was astonished and pleased. Well, well – to think of that monkey being clever enough to present Timmy with a biscuit that he very much wanted to eat himself! He wasn't a bad little thing! She went upstairs to find George and tell her.

But George didn't believe her. 'Timmy would never take a biscuit from that silly little monkey!' she said. 'Never! You made all that up, Joanna, just because you're getting fond of Mischief. You wait till he runs off with your toasting-fork again!'

All the same, George went down with Joanna, curious to see if the two animals *were* becoming friendly – and she saw a very strange sight indeed!

Mischief was on Timmy's back, and Timmy was solemnly trotting round the kitchen, giving him a ride! The monkey was chattering in delight, and Tinker was shouting in glee.

'Go faster, Tim, go faster! You're a very fine horse! You'd easily win the Derby! Go on, gallop!'

'I don't want Timmy to give rides to the monkey,' said George. 'Stop it, Timmy! You look silly.'

The monkey suddenly leaned forward and hugged Timmy round the neck. Then he slid off and looked at George as if to say, 'All right! I won't make your dog look silly!'

Timmy knew that George was cross and he went to lie down on the rug. At once Mischief came sidling across to him, and settled himself between Timmy's big front paws, cuddling there without fear. Timmy bent his big head and licked him very gently.

Tears came suddenly to Joanna's eyes. That Timmy! He

was just about the nicest dog in the whole world. 'See that!' she said to George. 'Big-hearted and kind that dog of yours is! Don't you scold him now for being great enough to make friends with a little creature who stole his bone!'

'I'm not *going* to scold him!' said George, astonished and proud. 'He's a marvel – the best dog in the world! Aren't you, Timmy darling?'

And she went over to Timmy and stroked his big soft head. He whined lovingly and licked her, looking up as if to say, 'Well, everything's all right now – we're *all* friends!'

Tinker had been watching from a corner of the kitchen, saying nothing. He was rather afraid of George and her quick temper. He was delighted when he saw her go over and pat Timmy, without even disturbing the monkey. In his joy he began to honk like a lorry, and startled everyone so much that they yelled at him:

'Stop it, Tinker!'

'Be quiet, you little nuisance!'

'Woof!' That was from Timmy.

'You'll have Mr Kirrin in here if you honk like that,' said Joanna. 'Can't you be something quiet for a change – a bicycle, for instance?'

Tinker thought that was quite a good idea. He ran round the kitchen and out into the hall, making a hissing noise like the sound of a bicycle's wheels on the road. Then he decided to make a noise like a bicycle bell, and produced a very loud ringing noise indeed! It was so like the ringing of a bell that Aunt Fanny ran out of the living room, thinking there was someone at the front door!

Then the study door flew open and out came Uncle Quentin and Tinker's father. Poor Tinker was caught, and his father shook him so hard that two pencils shot out of his pocket and rolled over the floor.

Tinker began to yell – and *how* he could yell! George came out of the kitchen to see what was happening, and Dick, Julian and Anne raced down the stairs. Joanna rushed out into the hall, too, and almost sent Uncle Quentin flying.

Then George did a very silly thing. She began to laugh – and when George laughed properly, her laugh was wonderful to hear! But neither Uncle Quentin nor Professor Hayling thought it wonderful – they merely thought it rude! George was laughing at *them* – and that wouldn't do at all!

'This is absolutely the last straw!' shouted Uncle Quentin, his face red with rage. 'First this boy ringing bells all over the place – and George encouraging him by laughing! I won't have it! Don't you know that very very important work is going on here, in Kirrin Cottage – work that may bring great benefits to the world! Fanny, send these children away somewhere. I won't have them in the house, disturbing us when we are doing such important work. Do you hear? SEND THEM AWAY! And that's my LAST word!'

And he and the professor stalked back to the study and banged the door. WELL! Now what was to be done?

CHAPTER FOUR

Tinker has a wonderful idea

AUNT FANNY had appeared during the row, and sighed when she heard her husband shouting. Oh, dear, dear – these scientists who liked to do wonderful things for the world – and yet often made their own families unhappy! She smiled at George's angry face, and took her arm.

'Come into the living room, dear, and bring the others with you. We'll have to decide what can be done. Your father really *is* doing wonderful work, you know – and I must say that Tinker and Mischief and Timmy don't help very much! All right, all right, George – I know it isn't Timmy's fault – but he does have a very loud bark, you know!'

She took the five children and Timmy into the living room. The monkey, scared at the shouting, had gone into hiding and was nowhere to be seen. Aunt Fanny called to Joanna.

'Joanna – come and help us to discuss what's to be done. This kind of thing can't go on.'

They all sat down, looking rather solemn. Timmy flopped down under the table, and put his nose on his paws. Where was that little monkey who had given him his biscuit?

TINKER HAS A WONDERFUL IDEA

The discussion began. George spoke first, most indignantly.

'Mother, this is our *home*. Why do we have to go away just because Father wants this scientist friend to stay with him? I have to do holiday homework, and I don't make a row every time Father bangs a door when I'm studying. But if I so much as . . .'

'That will do, George,' said her mother. 'You ought to understand your father better than you seem to. You are both exactly the same – impatient, short-tempered, bangers-of-doors, and yet both so kind, too! Now – let's see if we can find a way out.'

'I only wish we could stay at *my* home,' said Julian, feeling awkward. 'But it's all shut up, now that my parents have gone away.'

'Can't we take tents over to Kirrin Island?' said George. 'Yes, Mother, yes – I know what you're going to say – it's only the beginning of April, and it's far too cold and all the rest of it, and . . .'

'The forecast for the weather is very bad,' said her mother. 'Rain, rain, nothing but rain. You can't possibly go and camp in the pouring rain – and row to and fro, getting drenched each day – I'd have you all in bed with bronchitis before three days had gone – and *then* what should we do!'

'All right, Mother – have *you* any good suggestions?' said George, still cross.

'Hey – what's that monkey doing?' said Dick, suddenly. 'Stop him!'

'He's only poking the fire,' said Tinker. 'He thinks it's cold in here.'

'Well, what next!' said Joanna and took the poker firmly from the monkey's little paw. 'Do you want to set the house on fire, you – you little . . .'

'Monkey!' finished Dick, with a grin. 'I must say that Mischief is always up to mischief! Can't keep your eye off him for a moment!'

'Well, now – if we can't go to Kirrin Island, or back home, or stay here – where *can* we go?' said Julian, looking serious. 'Hotels are too expensive – and which of our friends would like to have five of us to stay, plus a wicked little monkey and a big dog with an enormous appetite?'

There was a silence. What a problem! Then suddenly Tinker spoke up.

'*I* know where we could go – and we'd jolly well have some fun, too!' he said.

'Oh – and where is this wonderful place?' asked George disbelievingly.

'Well – I was thinking of my lighthouse,' said Tinker, most surprisingly. And then, as no one said anything, but merely stared at him in astonishment, he nodded at them. 'I said my *lighthouse* – don't you know what a lighthouse is?'

'Don't be silly, please,' said Dick. 'This is no time for jokes.'

'It's *not* a joke,' said Tinker, indignantly. 'It's perfectly true. You ask my father.'

26

'But, Tinker dear – you can't possibly *own* a lighthouse,' said Aunt Fanny, smiling.

'Well, I do,' said Tinker, quite fiercely. 'You see, my father had some very special work to do, that couldn't be done on land – so he bought an old empty lighthouse, and did his work there. I went to stay with him – my, it was grand there, with the wind and the waves crashing about all the time.'

'But – surely he didn't *give* it to you, did he?' said Julian, disbelievingly.

'Yes, he did. Why shouldn't he, if I wanted it badly?' demanded Tinker. '*He* didn't want it any more, and nobody would buy it – and I wanted it terribly, so he gave it to me on my last birthday. And it's mine, I tell you.'

'Well, I'm blessed!' said Julian. 'Here's old George owning an island given to her by her mother – and Tinker owning a lighthouse given to him by his father! I wish my parents would present me with a volcano, or something really thrilling!'

George's eyes shone as she looked at the surprising Tinker. 'A lighthouse – of your very own! Where is it?'

'About twenty miles along this coast to the west,' said Tinker. 'It's not an awfully *big* one, you know – but it's smashing! The old lamp is still there, but it's not used now.'

'Why not?' asked Dick.

'Well, because a big new lighthouse was built farther along the coast, in a better position for warning ships,' explained Tinker. 'That's how it was this old one was put

27

up for sale. It was fine for my father to work in. Nobody ever disturbed him there – though he did get very angry with the seagulls sometimes. He said they mewed like great cats all the time, and made him feel he ought to put out milk for them.'

This made everyone burst into loud laughter, and Tinker sat beaming round proudly. How clever he must be to make these children laugh like that – yes, and even Joanna and Aunt Fanny too! He broke into their laughter by banging on the table.

'You do believe me now, don't you?' he said. 'It's quite true that the lighthouse is mine. You ask my father. Do let's all go and stay in it till our two fathers have finished their work. We could take Timmy and Mischief too – there's plenty of room.'

This proposal was so astonishing that no one answered for a few moments. Then George gave him a friendly dig in the chest.

'*I'll* come! Fancy living in a *lighthouse*! I bet the girls at school won't believe *that*!'

'Aunt Fanny! May we go?' said Anne, her eyes shining too.

'Well – I don't know,' said her aunt. 'It really is a most extraordinary idea. I shall have to discuss it with your uncle, and with Tinker's father too.'

'My father will say yes, I know he will!' said Tinker. 'We left some stores there – and some blankets – I *say*, wouldn't it be grand to run a lighthouse ourselves!'

TINKER HAS A WONDERFUL IDEA

The idea certainly appealed to all the Five – even Timmy thumped his tail on the floor as if he had understood every word. He probably had – he never missed anything that was going on!

'I've a map that shows where my lighthouse is,' said Tinker, scrabbling in one of his pockets. 'It's rather crumpled and dirty because I've looked at it so often. Look – here's a map of the coastline – and just there, built on rocks – is my lighthouse. It's marked by a round dot, look!'

Everyone pored over the grubby map. Nobody had the least doubt but that this was the answer to all their problems! Dick stared at the excited Tinker. How lucky he was to own a *lighthouse*! Dick had never before met a lighthouse owner – and to think it should be this funny little Tinker!

'The rocks that the lighthouse is built on used to wreck many ships,' said Tinker. 'Wreckers used to work along that coast, you know – they would shine a light as if to guide ships along the coast, and make them go on the rocks. Crash! They'd be broken to pieces, and everyone drowned – and the wreckers would wait till the ship was washed up on the shore, and then take everything they could from her.'

'The wicked wretches!' said Dick, horrified.

'There's a Wreckers' Cave there, too, where the wreckers stored the things they stole from the wrecked ships,' said Tinker. 'I haven't been very far into it – I'm too scared to. They do say there's an old wrecker or two there still.'

'Oh, nonsense!' said Aunt Fanny, laughing. 'That's probably just a tale to keep children away from dangerous caves and rocks. Well, dears – I really don't see any reason why you shouldn't go to Tinker's lighthouse, if his father agrees.'

'Mother! THANK YOU!' cried George, and gave her mother a hug that made her gasp. 'I *say* – living in an old *lighthouse* – it's too good to be true! I shall take my binoculars and keep watch for ships!'

'Well, Julian had better take his record-player as well,' said Mrs Kirrin. 'If it's stormy weather, it may be a bit duller than you think, cooped up in a lonely lighthouse!'

TINKER HAS A WONDERFUL IDEA

'It will be MARVELLOUS!' cried Tinker, and he suddenly became a racing car, tearing round the room at top speed, making a most extraordinary noise. Timmy barked and Mischief began to chatter loudly.

'Shush!' said Aunt Fanny. 'You'll make your father cross, Tinker, and that will be the end of your fine idea. Switch your engine off, please, and sit down quietly! I'll talk to your father as soon as I can!'

CHAPTER FIVE

Tinker's lighthouse

MRS KIRRIN thought that she might as well go immediately to the study, and see if her husband and Professor Hayling could talk about the children going away to this lighthouse of Tinker's. Could it really be true? She knocked discreetly at the closed door.

She could hear voices inside the room, but nobody called 'come in'. She knocked again.

'What is it NOW!' shouted Uncle Quentin. 'If it's you, George, go away and keep away. And if it's Tinker, tell him to go to the garage and park himself there. I suppose it's he who has been making all that row this morning!'

Aunt Fanny smiled to herself. Well, well – if all scientists were like her husband and Professor Hayling, it was a wonder they were ever calm enough to get any work done!

She went away. Perhaps she could bring up the subject of the lighthouse at dinner-time. What a relief it would be to have a peaceful house for a few days!

She went into the kitchen to find Joanna. The monkey was there, helping her! He had slipped away from Tinker and gone to see if there were any titbits about. Joanna was talking away to him as she rolled out pastry.

'See, I roll it like this – and like that – and I pick off a tiny bit for you!' And she gave Mischief a snippet for himself. He was very pleased, and leapt on Joanna's shoulder. He lifted a piece of her hair and whispered in her ear. Joanna pretended to understand.

'Yes, Mischief. If you're good I'll give you another titbit in a minute. Now get off my shoulder, and stop whispering. It tickles!'

'Well, Joanna – I never thought to see you rolling pastry with a monkey on your shoulder!' said Aunt Fanny. 'Joanna, what do you think about this lighthouse idea? I haven't been able to get into the study yet! My husband thought I was Tinker, and told me to go and park myself in the garage!'

'And a very good idea too,' said Joanna, rolling her pastry vigorously. 'Isn't that Tinker out in the hall now – sounds like a car of some sort! Well, I'd say that if the lighthouse is habitable, why shouldn't the Five go there, with Tinker and the monkey? They'd enjoy themselves all right, and Timmy would look after them. Sort of thing that they love – rushing off to a lighthouse! Ugh! Nasty lonely place, with waves crashing round and a wind fit to blow your head off!'

'Yes, but do you think they'd be all right all alone there, Joanna?' said Aunt Fanny.

'Well, Julian and Dick are old enough to look after the others – though I must say I wouldn't like the job of being in charge of that Tinker,' said Joanna. 'All I hope is that he doesn't imagine he's an aeroplane all of a sudden, and take off from the top of the lighthouse!'

Aunt Fanny laughed. 'Don't say that to *him*!' she said.
'His idea of being a car is bad enough. Well, Joanna, I feel
very mean sending George and the others away immediately they come here – but with two excitable scientists in
the house, I don't see that there's anything else to do.
Look out for that monkey – he's found your bag of
raisins!'

'Oh, you little mischief!' said Joanna, and made a grab
at the monkey. He shot off to the top of a cupboard with
the bag of raisins firmly held in one paw. He made a tiny
chattering noise, as if he were scolding Joanna.

'You come down with those raisins!' said Joanna,
advancing to the cupboard. 'Else I'll tie you to a chair
with that long tail of yours. You little monkey!'

Mischief said something in his funny little voice that
sounded rather cheeky. Then he put his paw into the bag
and took out a raisin. But he didn't eat it – he threw it
straight at Joanna! It hit her on the cheek, and she stared
at Mischief in astonishment.

'What! You'd pelt me with my own raisins! Well, that I
will NOT have!' She went to the sink and filled a cup with
water, while Mischief pelted both her and Aunt Fanny
with raisin after raisin! He danced about on the top of the
cupboard, screeching loudly in glee!

A bowl on the top of the cupboard fell off as the
monkey danced about, and crashed to the ground. The
noise scared him, and, with a flying leap, he shot off the
cupboard and landed on the top of the half-open door. He

34

pelted the two women from there, making the most extraordinary noises.

The study door was flung open, and out came Uncle Quentin, followed by the professor. 'What was that crash? What's happening here? How *can* we w . . .'

It was most unfortunate that Joanna should have thrown the cup of water at Mischief at that moment. He sat there on the top of the door – and the water fell all over him, splashed over the top of the door – and down on to Uncle Quentin's head as he pushed the door open!

Joanna was horrified. She disappeared into the scullery at once, not knowing whether to laugh or to make her apologies.

Uncle Quentin was astounded to find himself dripping wet. He stared angrily up at Mischief, absolutely certain that it was the monkey who had emptied the water over him.

By this time the Five had come out of the living room, wondering what the noise was. 'It's old Mischief,' said Tinker. 'Throwing water, I should think!'

'Well, actually, *I* threw the water,' began Joanna apologetically, peeping out of the scullery, 'because . . .'

'YOU threw it?' said Uncle Quentin, amazed. 'What *is* happening in this house? Things have come to a pretty pass if *you* start flinging water at people, Joanna. You ought to be ashamed of yourself! Are you mad?'

'Listen, Quentin,' said his wife. 'Nobody's mad at present, but pretty soon we all shall be, if this sort of thing goes on! Quentin, are you LISTENING? I've something important to say to you – and to you too, Professor.'

The professor remembered his manners. 'Please go on,' he said politely, and then flinched as a raisin hit him squarely on the head. Mischief had found one on the floor, and had taken a pot shot at the professor. Dick looked at the monkey admiringly – he really was a very good shot!

'What's that little idiot of a monkey throwing!' said Uncle Quentin, fiercely, and knew at once when a raisin hit him smartly on the nose. 'Get rid of him! Put him in the dustbin! Why have I to put up with monkeys that throw things and boys that chug about the house like cars gone mad? I tell you Fanny, I will NOT have it!'

Aunt Fanny looked at him very sternly. 'Listen Quentin, I have something to say. LISTEN! Tinker says his father gave him a lighthouse for his own, and he suggests that he and all the others should leave here and go and stay in the lighthouse. Quentin, are you listening?'

'A lighthouse! Are you mad? What, that little monkey of a boy says he owns a *lighthouse*? And you believed him?' said Uncle Quentin amazed.

'Tinker's quite right, as it happens,' said Professor Hayling. 'I bought a lighthouse to work in when I wanted to get right away from everywhere and concentrate – and when I'd finished, I couldn't sell it – so as Tinker pestered me for it, I gave it to him. But not to *live* in!'

'A *lighthouse* to work in!' said Uncle Quentin, thinking what a truly marvellous idea this was. 'I'll buy it from you! I'll . . .'

36

'No, Quentin, you won't do anything of the sort,' said his wife, firmly. 'Will you PLEASE listen to me, both of you. Professor Hayling, is the lighthouse fit for these five to stay in – and if so, they want to know if they can go there until you two have finished your work here. They're a nuisance to you – and to be quite honest, you're a nuisance to *them*!'

'Fanny!' said her husband, astonished and angry.

'Father, listen. We'll all get out of your way as soon as possible, if you'll say we can go to Tinker's lighthouse,' said George, planting herself firmly in front of her father. 'Say one word – 'YES' – that's all we want.'

'YES!' shouted Uncle Quentin, suddenly tired of all the argument, and longing to get back to his papers with the professor. 'YES! Go to the lighthouse – go to the Tower of London – go and live at the Zoo, if you like! The monkeys will welcome that mischievous little creature, sitting grinning up there on the cupboard! But go SOMEWHERE!'

'Oh, thank you, Father!' said George, joyfully.

'We'll go off to the lighthouse as soon as we can. HURRAY! THREE CH . . .'

But before she could continue, the study door shut with a bang behind the two exasperated men. George bent down, took Timmy's two front legs, and proceeded to dance all round the living room with him, shouting 'HURRAY! THREE CHEERS!' over and over again.

Aunt Fanny sat down suddenly in a chair, and began to laugh. Joanna laughed too. 'If we don't laugh, we shall cry!' she said. 'What a hullabaloo! Well, it's a good thing they'll soon be off. That loft is much too draughty for the boys, you know. Look at poor Julian – he's got such a stiff neck he can hardly turn it this morning.'

'Who cares?' said Julian. 'We'll soon be off again together, all the Five – and two more to keep us company. It will be quite an adventure!'

'An adventure?' said Tinker, surprised. 'But you can't have adventures in a lighthouse – it's out on the rocks, all by itself, as lonely as can be! There aren't any adventures to be found *there*!'

Ah – you wait and see, Tinker! You don't know the Five! If there's any adventure about, they're bound to be right in the middle of it!

CHAPTER SIX

Making plans

IT WAS very exciting making plans to go to the lighthouse. Tinker told them all about it, time and time again. 'It's very tall, and there's an iron stairway – a spiral one – going from the bottom up to the top. And at the top is a little room for the lamp that used to flash to warn ships away.'

'It sounds smashing,' said George. 'What about Timmy, though? Can he climb up a spiral stairway?'

'Well, he can live down at the bottom, can't he, if it's too difficult for him to climb up?' said Tinker. 'Mischief can climb it easily – he simply *races* up!'

'If Timmy has to live at the bottom, I shall live there with him,' said George.

'Why not wait and see the lighthouse before you arrange the sleeping places?' said Julian, giving her a friendly punch. 'Now first we must find out exactly where it is – and the way to get there. It's a pity Tinker can't turn into a *real* car – he could run us there in no time!'

Tinker at once imagined himself to be a large van, taking the Five and all their luggage along the road. He raced round the room, making his usual car noise, and hooting so loudly that he made everyone jump. Julian caught him as he raced round the table and sat him down firmly.

'Any more of that and we leave you behind,' he said. 'Now – where's that map of yours – let's have a look at it – and then we'll get Aunt Fanny's big map of the coast, and track down the road to your lighthouse.'

Soon Tinker and the Five were studying a large-scale map of the coast, Mischief sitting on Dick's shoulder and tickling his neck.

'See – that's the way to go,' said Julian. 'It really wouldn't be far by sea – look, round the coast here, cut across this bay, round the headland – and just there are the rocks on which the old lighthouse stands. But by road it's a very long way.'

'Better go by car, though,' said Dick. 'We've a good bit of luggage to take – not only our clothes, but crockery and things like that. And food.'

'There are still some stores there,' said Tinker, eagerly. 'Dad left some when we went away from the lighthouse.'

'They'll probably have gone bad,' said Julian.

'Well – don't take too much,' said Tinker. 'It's a pretty rough way over the rocks to the lighthouse – there isn't a road that runs right up to it, you know. We shall have to carry everything ourselves, once we get to the place. We can always get fresh food if we want it – the village isn't all that far away – but there are some days when you can't even leave the lighthouse! You see the waves splash house-high over the rocks when there's a rough wind. We'd have to get across by boat if the tide's in – the rocks are covered then!'

'This sounds too exciting for words!' said Dick, his eyes shining. 'What do *you* think about it, Anne? You haven't said a word!'

'Well – I do feel just a *bit* scared!' said Anne. 'It sounds so lonely. I do hope no ships will be wrecked on those awful rocks while *we're* there!'

'Tinker said there was a fine new lighthouse farther along the coast,' said Julian. 'Its light will keep every ship away from that wicked stretch of rocks. Look, Anne, you *would* like to come, wouldn't you? If not, Aunt Fanny wouldn't mind just *you* staying here – you're a little mouse, you wouldn't bother Uncle Quentin or the professor at all!'

'I shouldn't DREAM of not coming with you,' said Anne, indignantly. 'Julian – you don't think there are still wreckers about do you? I should hate that.'

'They belong to years gone by,' said Julian. 'Cheer up, Anne – this is just a little visit we're going to pay to Tinker's seaside house! He is kindly taking in visitors this spring!'

'Well, let's get on with our plans,' said Dick. 'We go there by car – er, *what* was that you just said, Tinker?'

'I said I'll drive you, if you like,' said Tinker. 'I could dr . . .'

'You haven't a driving licence, so don't talk nonsense,' said George, crossly.

'I know I haven't – but all the same I *can* drive!' said Tinker. 'I've driven my father's car round and round our garden, see? And . . .'

41

'Oh, do shut up,' said Dick. 'You and your pretend cars! Julian, when shall we go to his lighthouse?'

'Well, why not tomorrow morning?' said Julian. 'I'm sure everyone would be glad if we left as soon as possible! It's hard on Aunt Fanny and Joanna to have so many here. We'll see about a car and someone to drive us, and then we'll pack and make our getaway!'

'Hurray,' said George in delight, and pounded on the table, making Mischief leap up to the top of a bookcase in fright. 'Oh, sorry, Mischief – did I scare you? Timmy tell him I'm sorry, I didn't mean it. He probably understands your doggy language.'

Timmy looked up at Mischief, gave two little whines and a comforting wuff. Mischief listened with his head on one side, and then leapt down, landing neatly on Timmy's back.

'Thanks for giving him my message, Tim,' said George, and everyone laughed. Good old Timmy! He wagged his long tail and put his head on George's knee, looking up at her beseechingly.

'All right old thing – I understand your language, whether you talk with your voice or your eyes,' said George, patting him. 'You want a walk, don't you?'

'Woof!' said Timmy joyfully, and tore to the door.

'Let's walk down to the garage and see if they have a car or a van to hire out to us,' said Julian. 'We'll have to have a driver too, because someone has to take back the car. Come on, Timmy-dog!'

MAKING PLANS

They all set off to the garage in the village. The rain held
off for a while, and the sun came out, making Kirrin Bay
sparkle and shine.

'I wish we could have gone to stay on my island,' said
George. 'But it really is too damp to camp out. Anyway, a
lighthouse will be nice for a change!'

The man at the garage listened to Julian's tale of
wanting a car to go to the lighthouse. 'It's the old lighthouse at Demon's Rocks, not the new one at High Cliffs,'
he said. 'We're going to stay there.'

'Stay at a *lighthouse*!' said the man. 'This isn't a joke is
it?'

'No. It happens to belong to one of us,' said Julian. 'We
have a few things to take there, of course, and we hoped
you'd have a taxi tomorrow for us. We'd let you know
somehow when we are ready to come back from the
lighthouse, and you can send the same car for us then.'

'Right,' said the man. 'And you're staying at Kirrin
Cottage now, you say? Oh – your uncle is Mr Kirrin? Well,
I know Master George here, of course – but I wasn't
certain who *you* were. Some funny people order cars, you
know!'

George was pleased to be called *Master* George. It was
nice to be thought a boy. She dug her hands deep down in
the pockets of her jeans.

'We'd better take a few rugs and cushions,' said Julian.
'And some sweaters and wind-cheaters. I can't imagine it's
very warm in the lighthouse.'

43

'There's an oil-heater there,' said Tinker. 'I think it was for the lighthouse lamp when it was in use. We can use that for warmth, if we're cold.'

'What sort of stores did you and your father leave there?' asked Dick. 'We'd better order some foodstuffs at the grocer's – and some ginger beer or something – and take it all in the car.'

'Well – there's plenty of tinned food, I think,' said Tinker, trying to remember. 'We left it there in case my father wanted to come back at any time and work again in peace and quiet.'

'Hm. It's a pity he didn't fix up with Uncle Quentin to have him there with him,' said Julian. 'Then everyone would have been happy!'

They went to the grocer's and Anne tried her best to order what she thought they would need, outside of tinned food. 'Sugar – butter – eggs – oh dear – help me, George. How much shall I order?'

'Don't forget we *can* go shopping in Demon's Rocks village,' said Tinker. 'Only it's a bit of a nuisance if there's windy weather – the path over the rocks isn't very safe then. We might have to stay in the lighthouse for a day or two without leaving it. Even a boat might be too risky.'

'It sounds thrilling!' said George, picturing them all marooned by fierce storms, waiting to be rescued from peril and starvation! 'Get some biscuits, Anne. And bars of chocolate. And lots of ginger beer. And a big bottle of lemonade. And a . . .'

44

MAKING PLANS

'Wait a minute – do you know who's paying for all this?' said Julian. '*I* am. So don't ruin me completely!' He took out his wallet. 'Here's five pounds,' he said. 'That's all I can spare at present! Dick can buy the next lot of food we want!'

'Well, I've plenty of money too,' said Tinker, taking out a handful from his pocket.

'You would have!' said George. 'I suppose your father just hands out money whenever you ask him. He's so vague he wouldn't know if he paid you three times a day!'

'Well, *yours* seems pretty vague too,' said Tinker, smartly. 'He poured the coffee over his porridge this morning, instead of the milk. I saw him. And what's more, he ate it without even *noticing* it was coffee!'

'That's enough,' said Julian. 'We don't tell tales about our parents in public. Tinker, don't you want to take anything for Mischief to eat while we're in the lighthouse? George has bought biscuits for Timmy, and we're going to lay in a supply of bones, too.'

'I'll buy Mischief's food myself, thank you,' said Tinker, not very pleased at being ticked off by Julian. He gave an order for a packet of raisins, a packet of currants, a pound of apple rings and some oranges. Mischief eyed all these with very great *pleasure*.

'Paws off!' said George, sharply, as the little monkey slyly slid his paw into the bag of biscuits put ready for Timmy. Mischief jumped on to Tinker's shoulder and hid his face in his tiny paws, as if he were ashamed!

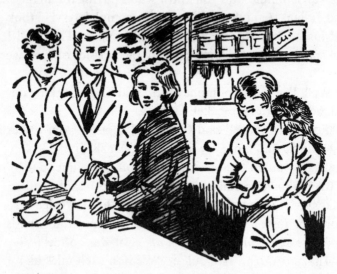

'We'll just buy some more fruit,' said Julian, 'and then I think we'll have enough. We'll take it all round to the garage, and put it in the car ready to take away tomorrow.'

'Tomorrow!' said George, her eyes shining. 'Oh, I hope it comes soon. I can't *wait* for it!'

CHAPTER SEVEN

Off at last!

IT WAS very exciting that evening to talk about the next day – the taxi coming to fetch them – the drive round the coast to Demon's Rocks – exploring the lighthouse – looking out over the endless sea, and watching the great waves coming in to pound on the rocks!

'What *I'm* looking forward to is our first night there,' said George. 'All alone, high up in that old lighthouse! Nothing but wind and waves around! Snuggling down in our rugs, and waking up to hear the wind and waves again.'

'And the gulls,' put in Tinker. 'They cry all the time. You can watch them from the lighthouse top. I wish I had wings like a gull – spread out wide – sitting on the wind as they glide!'

'Sitting on the wind – yes, that's exactly what they do!' said Anne. 'I just wish their cry didn't sound so mournful though.'

Aunt Fanny was half-inclined not to let the children go after all! The weather forecast was bad, and she pictured them sitting half-frozen, and perhaps very scared, in the old deserted lighthouse. But no sooner did she begin to wonder out loud if she ought to let them go than the children raised their voices in indignant chorus!

'But we've ordered the TAXI!'

'And heaps of food! And Joanna has packed up a big tin of all kinds of things. She even baked a special cake for us!'

'*Mother*! How *could* you think of saying no when you've already said yes!'

'All right, all right, dears!' said Aunt Fanny. 'I wouldn't really stop you going. But do send me a card or two, will you? That's if there's anywhere to post one!'

'Oh, there's a tiny post office in the village,' said Tinker. 'We'll send a card every day. Then you'll know we're all right.'

'Very well – but if a card doesn't come I'll be very worried,' said Aunt Fanny. 'So please do keep your word! You won't forget your anoraks will you – and your rubber boots, and . . .?'

'Mother! I feel as if you're going to mention *umbrellas* next!' said George. 'But honestly, we'd be blown out to sea if we put an umbrella up on Demon's Rocks. Tinker says there's always a gale blowing round the coast there.'

'You can think of us playing snap with our packs of cards, and having a fine time in the lighthouse while storms rage round and howl like demons!' said Dick. 'We'll be sitting snug in our rugs, with ginger beer beside us, and chocolate biscuits all round . . .'

'Woof,' said Timmy, at once, pricking his ears up at words he knew so well.

'Ha – you think you're going to feed on chocolate biscuits, do you, Tim?' said Dick, ruffling the dog's hairy

48

head. 'And please don't interrupt the conversation. It's not good manners.'

'Woof,' said Timmy apologetically, and licked Dick's nose.

'I think you'd all better go to bed early tonight,' said Aunt Fanny. 'You've still some packing to do tomorrow – and you say you've ordered the taxi for half past nine.'

'We'll be down to breakfast at eight o'clock sharp,' said Julian. 'I bet the professor won't be down till about eleven, and forget all about his bacon and eggs! Tinker, does your father *ever* have a really hot meal? I mean – it seems to me he either forgets them altogether, or wanders in hours late, and then doesn't know if he's having breakfast, dinner, or supper!'

'Well, I can always eat up everything that's there, if I think he's forgotten to come,' said Tinker, sensibly. 'Mischief helps too. You'd be surprised how fond Mischief is of fat bacon.'

'I'm not a *bit* surprised at anything Mischief does,' said Julian. 'I'm just wondering how we are going to put up with his tricks when we're all cooped up in the lighthouse together! We can't send him out into the garden then, to work off some of his high spirits. Aunt Fanny, do you know he took my pencil this morning and scribbled monkey words all over my wallpaper? It's a good thing I can't read monkey language for I'm sure he wasn't scribbling anything polite!'

'You're not to say things like that about Mischief,' said

49

Tinker, offended. 'He's very good-mannered for a monkey. You should see *some* monkeys I know!'

'I'd rather not, thanks,' said Julian.

Tinker was cross. He picked up Mischief and went out of the room. Soon there was the noise of a car out in the hall – one that needed repairing by the sound of it!

'R-r-r-r-RRRRRR-r-r-r-r, OOOOOOPH, Rrrrrrr, PARP!' Aunt Fanny rushed to the door. 'You *know* you've been told not to be a car out in the hall. Come back before your father hears you, Tinker. My goodness me, this house will be an entirely different place, once it is rid of all the cars that have driven about in it since you came!'

'I was only being a tractor,' said Tinker, surprised. 'I always feel as if I *must* go and be a car when people are horrid to me or Mischief.'

'Oh, be your age!' said George.

'I shall go up to bed,' said Tinker, offended again.

'Well, that's not a bad idea, seeing that you have to be punctual tomorrow morning,' said Aunt Fanny. 'Good night, then, Tinker dear. Good night, Mischief.'

Tinker found himself gently propelled to the door. He went up the stairs, grumbling, Mischief on his shoulder. But he soon stopped frowning as he undressed and thought of the next day. Off to the lighthouse – HIS lighthouse! Ha, that would make George and the others sit up. He snuggled down in bed with Mischief nestling beside him, one little paw down the front of Tinker's pyjama jacket.

OFF AT LAST!

Next morning George awoke first. She sat up, afraid that the weather forecast might be right, and that it would be pouring with rain. No – it was wrong for once – the sun shone down and she could not hear the sound of the sea – that meant that there was not much wind to blow up big waves that pounded on the shore.

She awoke Anne. 'Lighthouse day!' she said. 'Buck up – it's half past seven.'

They were all down very punctually to breakfast – except Professor Hayling! As usual he did not appear until breakfast was over, and then he sauntered in at the front door!

'Oh – you *are* up then,' said Aunt Fanny, 'I thought you were still asleep in bed.'

'No – Tinker woke me up at some very early hour,' complained the professor. 'Or else it was the monkey – I really don't know. They both look alike to me in the early morning.'

Uncle Quentin was already down, but hadn't come into breakfast. He was in his study as usual. 'George – go and fetch your father,' said Aunt Fanny. 'His breakfast will soon be inedible.'

George went to the study door and knocked. 'Father! Don't you want your breakfast?'

'I've had it!' said a surprised voice. 'Very nice – couple of boiled eggs.'

'Father! That was your *yesterday's* breakfast!' said George, impatiently. 'It's bacon and *fried* eggs today.

You've forgotten as usual. Do come. We're leaving for the lighthouse soon.'

'Lighthouse – what lighthouse?' said Uncle Quentin, in tones of great astonishment. But he had no answer, George had gone back to the dining room, not knowing whether to laugh or frown. Really! Father was so forgetful that he would forget where he lived next!

There was great excitement after breakfast. Rugs – coats – night clothes, the warmest that could be found – tins of cakes and mince-pies packed by Joanna – sandwiches to eat on the way – books – games – as George said, anyone would think they were going away for a month!

'The car's late!' said Dick, impatiently. 'Or else my watch is fast.'

'Here it comes!' said Anne, excited. 'Oh, Aunt Fanny, I wish you were coming too! We're going to have such fun! Where's Mischief – oh, there he is! And Timmy – Timmy, we're going to live in a lighthouse! You don't even know what that is, do you?'

The car came up to the front gate of Kirrin Cottage, and the driver blew his horn, making Uncle Quentin almost jump out of his skin. He turned on poor Tinker at once. 'Was that *you* up to your silly tricks of pretending to be a car, and hooting again? Own up, now!'

'No, it wasn't, on my honour it wasn't,' said Tinker indignantly, hopping out of the way of what looked as if it might be a very powerful slap. 'See – it's that car!'

'I'll just ask the driver what he means by driving up here

and hooting fit to scare us all!' said Uncle Quentin indignantly. 'What's he come here for, anyway?'

'FATHER! It's the TAXI that's come to take us to the LIGHTHOUSE!' said George, not knowing whether to laugh or be cross.

'Ah yes,' said Uncle Quentin. 'Why didn't you tell me before? Well, goodbye, goodbye! Have a good time, and don't forget to dry yourselves well after a bathe.'

They piled into the car, and the man put their luggage into the big boot. He stared as Timmy and Mischief leapt in. 'Sure you've all got enough room?' he said. 'What a carful!'

Then to the accompaniment of a loud R-r-r-r-RRR from the car's engine, and an equally loud one from the delighted Tinker, the car turned and drove away down the sandy lane.

'We're off,' said George, in a happy voice. 'Off all by ourselves again. It's the thing I like best of all. Do you like it too, Tim?'

'WOOF!' said Timmy, agreeing heartily, and lay down with his head on George's foot. Ah – now for a lovely holiday with George. Timmy didn't mind where he went – even to the end of the world – so long as he was with George!

CHAPTER EIGHT

There's the lighthouse!

ONCE THEY were out on the main road, Tinker began to talk to the driver, asking him questions about all kinds of cars. The others listened, amused.

'Well, I don't think much of the new cars,' said Tinker. 'All gadgets!'

'Some of the new gadgets are very good,' said the driver, amused with the cocky little boy, and he touched a little lever beside him. At once the window next to Tinker went down smoothly, with a curious low moan. Tinker was extremely startled.

'Oh, don't open that window,' said Anne, as a rough wind swooped in. 'For goodness sake shut it, Tinker.'

Tinker shut it and began to talk about cars again. Once more the driver touched the lever beside him, and once more Tinker's window slid mournfully down, and a cold draught came in.

'TINKER! Don't mess about with the windows,' ordered Julian.

'I never touched the thing,' said Tinker, eyeing the window with suspicion. It suddenly shut itself, sliding upwards very smoothly. Tinker began to feel uncomfortable. He watched the window closely, afraid that it might play tricks again. The others, knowing perfectly well that the driver could open and shut any of the windows automatically from his own seat, nudged one another, and giggled. 'That shut up poor old Tinker!' murmured Dick.

It had. Not another word about new cars or old came from Tinker during the whole drive! It was a very pleasant one, mostly round the coast, and very little inland. The views were magnificent.

'That dog of yours seems to like the views,' said the driver. 'His head has been out of the window all the time.'

'Well – I always thought it was because he liked the fresh air,' said George. 'Timmy, is it because you enjoy the views?'

'Woof,' said Timmy, and withdrew his head to give George a lick. He also gave the little monkey a lick. Poor Mischief didn't much like the motion of the car. He sat very still indeed, afraid that he might be sick. The car purred along, sounding just like Tinker's usual imitation!

They stopped for an early lunch, and ate their sandwiches hungrily, sitting on a cliff. The driver had brought his own, and once Mischief had discovered that half the man's sandwiches were made of tomato, he sat on his knee in a very friendly manner, sharing his sandwiches in delight.

'We'll be there in about ten minutes,' said the man. 'Where are you staying at Demon's Rocks? The garage didn't tell me.'

THERE'S THE LIGHTHOUSE!

'At the lighthouse,' said Julian. 'Do you know it?'

'Yes – but people don't *stay* there!' said the driver, thinking that Julian was pulling his leg. 'What hotel are you going to – or are you staying with friends?'

'No. We really *are* going to the lighthouse,' said Tinker. 'It's mine. My very own.'

'Well – you're certainly got a place with a fine view!' said the driver. 'I was born at Demon's Rocks. My old great-grandad is still in the same cottage where I was born. My word – the stories he used to tell me of that old lighthouse – and how the wreckers got into it one night and grabbed the keeper there, and doused the light, so that a great ship might go on the rocks.'

'How horrible – and *did* it get wrecked?' asked Dick.

'Yes. Smashed to bits,' said the driver. 'Ab-so-lutely – smashed – to bits! And then they waited for the tide to wash up the wreckage. You ought to look up my old great-grandad, and get him to tell you his tales. He might even show you the Wreckers' Cave . . .'

'Oh – we heard about that,' said George. 'Is it really true – *can* we see it? And is there someone in there still?'

'No – no, all the old wreckers are gone long ago,' said the driver. 'As soon as the new lighthouse was built, the wreckers' day was done. It's so powerful, you see. Its beams can be seen even in the fiercest storm. The beam from the lighthouse you're going to wasn't very good – but it saved a good many ships, all the same!'

'What's your great-grandad's name?' asked George,

making up her mind to look him up as soon as she could. 'Where does he live?'

'Ask for Jeremiah Boogle,' said the driver, carefully skirting a herd of cows. 'You'll find him sitting somewhere on the quay, smoking a long pipe, and scowling at anyone that comes near him. But he likes children, so don't you be afraid of his scowl. He'll tell you a few tales, will my old great-grandad! Well, bless us all, if there isn't *another* herd of cows coming round the corner.'

'Hoot at them,' said Tinker.

'Ever heard the rhyme about the cow that jumped over the moon, boy?' said the driver. 'Well, someone hooted when it came by, see? And that's what it did – jumped over the moon! No good driver hoots at cows. It scares them silly, and they jump like hares. Look – see that cliff round the curve of the coast there? Well, that's the first bit of Demon's Rocks. We'll soon be there now.'

'Why is it called that?' asked George.

'Well, the rocks there are so wicked that it was reckoned they could only have been put there by some kind of savage demon,' said the driver. 'Some are just below the water so that they catch the keel of a boat and rip it. Others stick up sharp as sharks' teeth – and there's a great ledge of rocks where a boat can be pounded to bits by the waves. Ah, they're Demon's Rocks all right!'

'When shall we see the lighthouse?' asked Tinker. 'We ought to see it soon.'

'Wait till another bit of the coast comes in sight as soon

58

as we get to the top of this hill,' said the driver. 'And just tell that monkey of yours to take his paw out of my coat pocket. I've no more tomatoes there!'

'Behave yourself, Mischief,' said Tinker, so sternly that the little creature hid its face in its paws and whimpered.

'Little humbug!' said George. 'There's not a *tear* in his eye! Oh look – is *that* the lighthouse?'

'Yes. That's it,' said the driver. 'You get a good view of it now, from this hill. Fine one isn't it, for an old one? Ah, they could build well in those days. That one's made of stone. It's wave-swept so it has to be fairly tall, or the shining of the lamp would have been hidden by the spray falling on the windows.'

'Where did the lighthouse keeper live?' asked Dick.

'Oh, there's a cosy enough room just under the lamp room,' said the driver. 'My grandad took me up there once. I never saw such a view of a stormy sea in my life!'

'My father lived there all one summer,' boasted Tinker. 'I was with him most of the time. It was grand.'

'Why did your father want to live in a lighthouse?' asked the driver, curiously. 'Was he hiding, or something?'

'Of course not. He's a scientist, and he said he wanted peace and quiet, with no telephones ringing, and no one coming to see him,' said Tinker.

'And do you mean to say he had peace and quiet with *you* there?' said the driver teasingly. 'Well, well!'

'It's not so quiet there really,' said Tinker. 'The waves make such a noise, and so does the wind. But my father didn't really notice those. He only notices things like bells ringing, or people talking, or somebody knocking at the door. Things like that drive him mad. He loved the lighthouse.'

'Well – I hope you enjoy yourselves there,' said the driver. 'It's not my cup of tea – hearing nothing but waves and gulls crying. Better you than me!'

They descended the other side of the hill and the lighthouse was no longer to be seen. 'Soon be there now,' said Tinker. 'Mischief, will you like to be at the lighthouse again? How quickly you could go up the spiral staircase and down – do you remember?'

The car swept down almost to the edge of the sea. The lighthouse was now plainly to be seen, a good way out from the shore. A small boat bobbed at a stone jetty, and Tinker pointed it out with a scream of joy. 'That's the boat we had – the one that took us to and from the lighthouse when the tide was in! It's called *Bob-About*, and it does bob about too.'

'Is it yours?' asked George, rather jealously.

'Well, it was sold with the lighthouse, so I suppose it is,' said Tinker. 'Anyway, it's the one we'll use when we can't wade over the rocks.'

'Well, see you don't get storm-bound in the lighthouse,' said the driver, bringing the car to a stop. 'The sea between Demon's Rocks and the jetty will be too rough for that little boat, in stormy weather.'

'I can manage boats all right,' said George. 'I've had one

since I was small.'

'Yes. You're pretty good with them, that I do know,' said the driver. 'Well – here we are. Are you going to go straight to the lighthouse – in that boat? Shall I help you carry your things to it?'

'Well, thanks,' said Julian, and between them they carried everything to the little boat. An old man sat nearby, and he touched his cap to them. 'Message came through from Kirrin to say I was to get the old boat out for you,' he said. 'Which of you's Master Hayling?'

'I am,' said Tinker. 'And that's *my* boat, and *that's* my lighthouse! Come on, everyone – let's row to the lighthouse – come on! I can hardly wait to get there!'

CHAPTER NINE

Inside the lighthouse!

THE FIVE children jumped down into the boat, which was certainly acting up to its name of *Bob-About*! Timmy leapt in after George, but Mischief the monkey cried in terror when Tinker took him into the bobbing boat and sat down, holding him firmly.

'It's all right, Mischief,' said Tinker. 'Don't you remember this little boat of mine? You never did like going in a boat, though, did you?'

There were two pairs of oars. Julian took one pair, and George was going to take the other, when Dick quietly took them himself, grinning at George's angry face.

'Sorry – there's a good old swell on the sea, and we've to row through some pretty good waves. I'm just a *bit* stronger than you, George!'

'I row *just* as well as you do,' said George. The boat gave a great roll to one side just then, and she just managed to save one of their suitcases from toppling overboard.

'Well saved!' said Julian. 'And only just in time too! What a swell there is just here!'

'Are you going to row right over the rocks?' asked Anne peering down into the water. 'They are covered by the water now – we shan't scrape the bottom of the boat at all.'

'These are the rocks that we can walk over when the tide's out,' said Tinker. 'Lovely pools there are in them, too! I used to wallow in a nice warm one that was so well-heated by the sun that I wished I had a cold tap to turn on when the water felt too hot!'

Anne chuckled. 'I wish it was warm enough to bathe now,' she said. 'My word – look down and see what horrible rocks there are, just beneath the boat!'

'Yes – I bet they ripped up many a poor ship in the old days,' said Julian. 'No wonder they called them Demon's Rocks! It's a bit of a pull over them, isn't it, Dick?'

'Let *me* have a turn,' said George, grabbing at one of Dick's oars.

'Nothing doing,' said Dick, with a grin. 'You just look after those bags, old thing!'

'Is it a very *old* lighthouse?' asked Anne, as they swung over the hidden rocks, and the lighthouse came nearer and nearer. 'It *looks* old!'

'Yes, it is,' said Tinker. 'It's an odd little lighthouse, really – built by a rich man years and years ago. His daughter was drowned in a ship that was wrecked on these rocks – so he built a lighthouse, partly as a memorial to the girl, and partly to prevent other shipwrecks.'

Anne gazed at it. It was sturdily built and seemed very tall to her. Its base was firmly embedded in the rocks below it. Dick thought that the foundations must go very deep down into the rocks, to hold the lighthouse firmly in the great gales that must blow in bad weather. A gallery, rather like a verandah, ran round the top, just below the windows through which the lighthouse lamp once shone. What a view there would be from that gallery, thought Anne.

They came near to the lighthouse, which had stone steps running from the rocks up to a doorway built some way above the crashing waves.

'Will the door be locked?' asked Dick, suddenly. 'I wouldn't want to row all this way and then find we can't get into the place!'

'Of course the door will be locked,' said Tinker. 'Any-one got the key?'

INSIDE THE LIGHTHOUSE!

'Oh, don't be a donkey!' said Julian, resting his oars, and glaring at Tinker. 'Do you mean to say we can't get in, after all this?'

'It's all right!' said Tinker, grinning at Julian's dismayed face. 'I just wanted to pull your leg. Here's the key! It's *my* lighthouse, you see, so Dad gave me the key, and I always carry it about with me. It's very precious.'

It was an extremely large key, and George marvelled that Tinker could keep it in his pocket. He flourished it at them, grinning again. 'I'm looking forward to unlocking *my* lighthouse with *my* key!' he said. 'I bet *you* wish you had a lighthouse of your own, George.'

'Well, yes, I do,' said George, gazing up at the towering lighthouse, now so near to them.

'You'd better be a bit careful now,' said Tinker to the boys. 'Wait till a big waves swells up, then ride over it, and make for that rock over there – the one standing out of the water. There's a calm bit beyond it, for some reason, and you can row up to the steps quite safely. Look out for a stone post there, and chuck the rope round it, George. You're in a better position than I am for that.'

It was all done much more easily than the Five hoped. The boat swung into a stretch of fairly calm water, and the two boys rowed hard for the steps. George neatly threw the loop of rope over the post – and there they were, at the foot of the lighthouse, with only a few rocks to climb over to reach the steps. These rocks were not under water, and one by one the children and Timmy jumped out, and stared up at the lighthouse. It seemed much bigger now that they were just at the bottom!

'I'll unlock the door,' said Tinker, proudly, and climbed up the steep stone steps. 'Look at the enormous great stones that my lighthouse is made of. No wonder it has stood so long!'

He thrust the great key into the lock of the stout wooden door, and tried to turn it. He struggled for a minute, and then turned to the others with a scared face. 'I can't open the door!' he said. '*Now* what do we do?'

'I'll have a try,' said Julian. 'It's probably stuck.' He took hold of the key, gave it a strong twist – and opened the door! Everyone was most relieved. Julian pushed the others in out of the wind and the spray, and shut the door firmly.

'Well – here we are!' he said. 'Isn't it dark! Good thing I brought a torch!'

He shone the torch round, but all that was to be seen was a steep iron staircase spiralling up the middle of the lighthouse!

'The staircase goes right up to the top, to the lamp-room,' explained Tinker. 'It passes through a few rooms on the way. I'll show you. Hang on to the railing of the staircase, you may feel giddy going up round and round so steeply.'

Tinker proudly led the way up the steep little staircase, that went round and round and round! They came to a hole through which the stairway passed into a little dark

room. 'One of the storerooms,' said Tinker, and flashed his torch round. 'See – there are tins of food that I told you my father and I left here. Now we go on up to the oil-room

– that's not very big.'

'What's the oil-room?' asked Anne.

'Oh it was just where tins of paraffin oil used to be kept – the oil they used for the light at the top of the lighthouse. The old lamp had to burn oil, you see – there wasn't electricity in those days. Look – here's the oil-room.'

The oil-room had a very low ceiling, no window, and was packed with old tins. It had a nasty smell, and Anne held her nose with her fingers.

'I don't like this room,' she said. 'It has a horrid smell and a horrid *feel* about it! Let's go on up the staircase.'

The next room had one of the few little windows in the lighthouse, and as the sun came through it, it was much lighter and more cheerful.

'This was where my father and I slept,' said Tinker. 'Look, we forgot to take that old mattress away with us. What a bit of luck! We can use it!'

Up the spiral staircase they went once more, and this time they came to a room with a higher ceiling than the others, and a good window, though small. The sun came through this one too, and it looked quite homely! It had a table, and three chairs, and a box. It also had an old desk, and a little paraffin stove for boiling water or frying food.

'There's my old frying-pan!' said Tinker. 'We'll find that jolly useful. And a kettle – and a saucepan. And we left spoons and forks and knives behind, though not enough for all five of us, I'm afraid. And there's crockery too – though not as much as there ought to be. I broke rather a lot. But there are some tin cups and plates – I used just to wipe them clean with a cloth. Water's precious in a lighthouse you know.'

'Where is the water tank?' asked George. 'We'll have to have some water.'

'My father arranged a catch-tank on the west side of the lighthouse,' said Tinker, proudly. 'It catches rainwater, and runs into a pipe that goes through one of the windows and fills a little tank over a sink. I forgot to show you that. There's a tap to turn the water on and off. My father's very clever you know – and a thing like that is as simple as ABC. He didn't want to have to fetch water every day for washing in! Gosh, we did have fun here!'

'Well, it looks as if you'll have some *more* fun!' said Dick. 'You've plenty of company this time! You must have been jolly lonely before.'

'Oh, well – I had Mischief,' said Tinker, and when he heard his name, the little monkey came scampering over to him, and leapt into the boy's arms, cuddling into him lovingly.

'And what's the next room in this marvellous little lighthouse?' asked Julian.

'There's only one more – and that's the lamp-room. I'll show you that – it used to be the most important room in the place – but now it's lonely – never used – quite forgotten! Come and see!' And up the last spiral of the stairway went Tinker. How very, very proud he was of his lighthouse!

CHAPTER TEN

Settling in

ONCE MORE they all climbed up the spiral stairway, Timmy rather slowly, for he found the winding stairs difficult. Mischief shot up in front of them, almost as if *he* were the owner of the lighthouse, and was showing off his home!

The lamp-room was a high room with big windows all round it. It was very bright, for the sun shone steadily into it. The view was magnificent!

Anne gave a shout of wonder. The lighthouse was so high that the children could see for miles and miles over the heaving dark blue sea. They went all round the lamp-room, looking in every direction.

'Look! There's a door here!' cried Dick. 'Does it open on to that little balcony, or gallery, or whatever it is that runs all round this room?'

'Yes. The gallery goes completely round the lamp room,' said Tinker. 'You should see it sometimes when the weather's rough, and the gulls go seeking somewhere out of the storm. They perch on that gallery by the dozen! But you can't go out there except in calm weather – you might be blown right off! You've no idea what it's like when there's a storm. Honestly, one night when my father and I were here I thought I felt the lighthouse rocking!'

'This is about the most exciting place I've ever stayed in,' said Anne, her eyes shining. 'Tinker, I think you are the luckiest boy in the world!'

'Do you really?' said Tinker, pleased. He gave Anne a little pat. 'I hoped you'd like it. Mischief loves it – don't you, Mischief?'

Mischief was up on top of the great lamp. He chattered down to Timmy as if he were telling him all about it. Timmy listened, his ears cocked, his head on one side.

'He looks just as if he understood that monkey-gabble!' said George. 'Tinker – this lamp is never lit now, is it?'

'No, never,' said Tinker. 'I told you there is a fine new lighthouse a bit farther down the coast. It has a terrific lamp – run by electricity. We shall see its beams sweeping the sea at night.'

'Why don't people build lighthouses and live in them?' wondered George, as she gazed out over the wide blue sea.

'Anyone feeling hungry?' asked Tinker, rubbing his tummy. 'I feel jolly empty. Oh gosh – we haven't taken the things out of my boat! Come on – let's carry them all indoors, and have a meal. What's the time? Past four o'clock! No wonder I feel empty. Come on, Mischief – to work! You can carry some of the things in too.'

They ran down the spiral stairway, through room after room, and came to the great door. 'I suppose it had to be built as thickly and strongly as possible, because of the sea dashing against it in storms,' said Julian, pulling it open. The wind rushed in and almost knocked him over! They pushed their way out, and climbed back over the rocks to where they had left the boat. It was bobbing gently up and down in the little stretch of calm water.

'Hallo, *Bob-About*!' said Tinker. 'Did you think we were never coming? Got all our goods safely? Good little boat!'

'Idiot!' said Dick, grinning. 'Come on, Ju – I'll take half the heavy things, you take the rest. The girls and Tinker can manage the smaller things. Hey, Mischief, what do you think you're doing?'

Mischief had picked up a parcel or two, and was bounding off with them. 'It's all right! He's used to helping!' shouted Tinker. 'He often goes shopping with me, and carries bags and things. Let him help, he likes it.'

The monkey certainly was very useful. He scampered to and fro with all kinds of little things, and chattered happily. Timmy stood staring at him, his tail down, wishing he could use his paws as nimbly as Mischief could. George gave him a loving pat.

'It's all right, Timmy, darling. Here – take this basket.'

Timmy took the basket in his mouth by the handle and leapt happily up the steps of the lighthouse. He might not be able to pick up the little things that Mischief so easily managed – but at least he could carry baskets!

'We'll leave the boat bobbing up and down,' said Tinker. 'It will be quite all right there, tied to the post, unless the sea gets terribly rough – then we'll have to pull it halfway up the steps.'

'Let's have our meal and unpack before we arrange our things,' said Anne. 'I really do feel very hungry now. What sort of a meal shall we have? I feel as if I want something more than a tea-time meal!'

'That's the worst of living in a lighthouse,' said Tinker, quite seriously. 'You're awfully hungry nearly all the time. I used to have five or six meals a day when I stayed here with my father.'

'Sounds all right to *me*,' said Dick, with a grin. 'Let's have a "tea-sup" meal, shall we? A mixture of tea and supper! Tea-sup!'

Some of the things were put into the bedroom and some into the living room. Soon Tinker popped a saucepan of water on the stove to boil. Because of the rainy weather, the little rain catch-tank had provided plenty of water for the small inside tank set over the sink, which was most conveniently put in the living room. When Tinker turned on the tap, out came clear rainwater!

'Magic!' said Anne, delighted. 'I feel as if I'm in a dream!'

Eggs were put into the saucepan, and were soon boiled. 'Exactly three minutes and a half,' said Anne, ladling out each one with a spoon. 'TWO eggs each! At this rate we shall have to go shopping every day! George, you cut some bread-and-butter. The bread's in that bag – but goodness knows where the butter is. I know we bought some.'

'What about having a few of Joanna's famous mince pies too?' said Dick, taking the lid off a big square tin. 'Whew! Dozens! And cherry buns as well! And home-made macaroons – Joanna's speciality! I *say* what a meal!'

'What shall we have to drink?' said Julian. 'Ginger beer? Lemonade? Or shall we make some tea?'

Everyone voted for ginger beer. It was a very pleasant and cheery meal that the Five had in the old lighthouse, with Mischief and Tinker. The gulls called outside, the wind gave the lighthouse an occasional buffet, and the sound of the sea was mixed with all the other noises – lovely! Anne hugged her knees as she waited for her ginger beer. To think they were going to stay here for days and days. All by themselves.

When the meal was over, Anne and George washed up

in the little sink. 'Oh don't wash up – just give the things a quick wipe-over!' said Tinker. 'Like this!'

'Oh *no*!' said Anne. 'That's just like a boy! You'd better leave this side of things to me. I *like* doing jobs like this, see?'

'Just like a girl!' said Tinker, with a grin.

'No, it isn't,' said George. 'I hate doing them, and *I'm* a girl – though I wish I wasn't!'

'Never mind – you *look* like a boy, and you're often as *rude* as a boy, and you haven't an awful lot of manners,' said Tinker, quite thinking that he was comforting George.

'I've more manners than *you*,' said George, and stalked off in a huff to look out of the windows. But nobody could be in a huff for long, with that wonderful view – sea for miles and miles, tipped here and there with white breakers. George gave a sigh of pleasure. She forgot that she was annoyed with Tinker, and turned to him with a smile.

'If I could own this view, I'd feel I was the richest person in all the world!' she said. 'You're very lucky, Tinker.'

'Am I?' said Tinker, thinking it over. 'Well, you can have half the view, if you like. I don't want it all.'

Julian laughed, and clapped the boy on the back. 'We'll all share it, while we're here!' he said. 'Come on – let's unpack and arrange everything. Girls, you had better sleep here in this living room – and we three boys will sleep down in the bedroom. That all right by you, Tinker?'

'Fine – so long as you don't mind Mischief sleeping with

us,' said Tinker. 'Anyway I expect Timmy will sleep with the girls.'

'Woof,' said Timmy, agreeing. He was certainly not going to sleep anywhere without George!

They all had fun unpacking, and putting the things in the different places. 'Storeroom for that,' Julian said, 'and living room for this and this – and bedroom for these rugs – though these two had better go to the living room, because the girls will sleep there.'

'Cards for the living room,' said Dick, handing them to Anne. 'And books. And papers. Gosh, we mustn't forget to send a card each day to Aunt Fanny. We promised we would.'

'Well, she'll know we arrived safely today because the taxi driver will be sure to send a message to her,' said George. 'But tomorrow we'll go down to the village and buy a stock of postcards – and we'll send one every single day. I know Mother will worry if we don't.'

'All mothers are worriers,' said Dick. 'It's a nuisance – but on the other hand it's one of the nice things about them. Now then – what about a game of cards?'

And there they all are in the lighthouse, playing cards with shouts and laughter, Timmy and Mischief watching. You do have fun together, Five, don't you?

CHAPTER ELEVEN

Jeremiah Boogle

WHEN IT began to get dark, Tinker left the card table, and fetched an old-fashioned oil-lamp. He shook it.

'It's still got some oil in,' he said. 'Good. I'll light it, then we can see properly.'

'What a pity we can't light the great oil-lamp at the top of the lighthouse,' said George. 'That must have been the lighthouse keeper's great moment – lighting up the lamp to warn ships away. I wonder who first thought of a lighthouse – someone whose folk sailed, and might be wrecked on rocks, I suppose?'

'One of the first great lighthouses was built ages ago on an island called Pharos at the mouth of the Nile, not far from the great port of Alexandria,' said Julian.

'What was it built of – stone, like this one?' asked Tinker.

'No. It was built of white marble,' said Julian. 'I thought of it today when we went up the spiral staircase here – because the Pharos lighthouse had one too – much, much bigger than ours.'

'What was their lamp like?' asked Tinker.

'I don't know if it had a *lamp*,' said Julian. 'It's said that an enormous fire was built each night on the top of the

lighthouse, whose flames could be seen by ships a hundred miles away!'

'Goodness – it must have been a pretty high lighthouse, then, this Pharos!' said Dick.

'Well, it was supposed to be about 180 metres high!' said Julian.

'Whew! I wonder the wind didn't blow it down!' said Dick. 'Let's go and see it one day – if it's still there.'

'Idiot!' said Julian. 'It's gone long since. After all, it was built over twenty-two hundred years ago! An earthquake

79

came along one day and the magnificent lighthouse was shaken to bits – completely destroyed!'

There was a shocked silence. Everyone looked round at the walls of the lighthouse they were in. An earthquake! What a catastrophe that would be for even a *little* lighthouse!

'Cheer up, Anne!' said Julian, with a laugh. '*We're* not likely to be visited by an earthquake tonight! That old lighthouse on Pharos Island was one of the Seven Wonders of the Ancient World. No – *don't* ask me the others – I'm getting too sleepy to remember!'

'I wish we could light the lamp in *this* lighthouse,' said Anne. 'It can't like being a *blind* lighthouse, after shining brightly for so many years. *Could* the lamp be lit, Tinker, or is it broken now?'

'Anne – if you think we're going to scramble round that lamp-room and light the lamp just because you feel sorry about it, you're mistaken,' said Dick, firmly. 'Anyway, it's sure to be out of order after all these years.'

'I don't see why it should be,' objected Tinker. 'The lamp's never been interfered with.'

'Look – are we going to go on with our game, or are we not?' said Julian. 'I may as well remind you that I have won practically every game so far! Unless someone else wins a game soon I shall consider that I'm playing with a bunch of nitwits!'

That was quite enough to make everyone pick up their cards, and see if they couldn't possibly beat Julian!

'We'll jolly well play till you're well and truly beaten!' said Dick.

But no – nobody could beat Julian that night. Luck went his way all the time. At the end of the fifth game Anne yawned loudly.

'Oh, sorry!' she said. 'Don't think I'm bored. That yawn came too suddenly for me to stop it!'

'Well, I feel decidedly yawny too,' said Dick. 'What about a snack of something – and then we'll go to bed. We had such an enormous tea-sup that I feel I can't manage another *meal* – but a chocolate biscuit or two would be quite welcome.'

'Woof!' said Timmy at once, agreeing heartily, and Mischief said something in his little chattering voice, and tugged at Tinker's sleeve.

'I'll bring you a snack or two,' said Anne, getting up. She soon came back with a tray on which she had put lemonade, large slices of Joanna's new cake, and a chocolate biscuit for everyone, including Timmy and Mischief.

They ate with enjoyment, feeling lazy and comfortable. 'And now to bed!' said Julian. 'Girls, do you want any help with your mattress or rugs or anything?'

'No, thanks,' said Anne. 'Do you boys want to wash, and clean your teeth at the sink here? Because if so, do it now.'

Before a quarter of an hour had gone, everyone was bedded down comfortably. The three boys curled up in rugs in the bedroom below, with Mischief cuddled into

Tinker's neck. The two girls and Timmy lay on a mattress, with a blanket over them, Timmy lay beside George, occasionally licking her ear with his big tongue.

'*Dear* Timmy!' said George, sleepily. 'I love you – but do please keep your tongue to yourself!'

And soon they were all asleep, boys, girls, and animals too. Outside, the sea sighed and splashed and swirled, and the wind cried like the daytime gulls. But all was peace and quiet inside the old lighthouse. Not even Mischief the monkey stirred in his sleep.

It was fun to wake up in the morning, and hear the gulls screaming round; fun to have breakfast of eggs and bread and butter, and apples to crunch afterwards – fun to plan what to do that day.

'I vote we do a bit of shopping and buy some more eggs, and fresh bread, and a bottle or two of creamy milk,' said Anne.

'And we might try and find the taxi driver's great-grandad, and ask him a few things about the lighthouse, and the wreckers that came in the old days,' said Dick.

'Yes – and he might show us the Wreckers' Cave!' said Julian. 'I'd like to see that! Let's buck up with whatever jobs there are to do, and we'll go over the rocks to the jetty. The tide should be out, so we ought to be able to walk over.'

'Well, we *must* be back before the tide comes in, then,' said Tinker. 'Because if we leave the boat tied up here by

the lighthouse, we shan't be able to get back once the sea sweeps over the rocks and cuts us off!'

'Right,' said Julian. 'Be ready as soon as you can.'

Everyone was ready very quickly, and the little party set off over the rocks that at low tide lay between the lighthouse and the shore. Wicked rocks they were too – with sharp edges and points that would hole a ship at once!

Soon the children were on the little stone jetty. 'What was the name of old Great-Grandad?' said Dick frowning.

'Jeremiah Boogle,' said Anne. 'And he smokes a long pipe, and scowls at people.'

'Well – he *should* be easy to find!' said Julian. 'Come along. He's probably somewhere on the quay.'

'There he is!' said George, spotting an old man with a long pipe in his mouth. 'That's Jeremiah, I'm sure!'

Yes, there he was, sitting with his legs stretched out in front of him, an old, old man, smoking a very long pipe! He had a fine beard, a yachting cap askew on his head, and such enormous shaggy eyebrows that it was difficult to see his eyes beneath them!

The Five went up to him, with Timmy trotting behind, and Mischief on Tinker's shoulder. The old man spotted Mischief at once.

'Well, well – a monkey!' he said. 'Many's the little monkey I've brought home from my voyages.' He snapped his fingers and made a curious noise in his throat. Mischief stared at him, listening. Then he leapt from Tinker's shoulder on to the old man's, and rubbed his head against the old sailor's hairy ear.

'Mischief!' said Tinker, amazed. 'Look at that, George. He never goes to a stranger!'

'Well, maybe I knew his great-grandfather!' said the old sailor, laughing, and scratching Mischief's neck.

'All monkeys like me – and I like them!'

'Er – are you Mr Jeremiah Boogle?' asked Julian.

'Jeremiah Boogle, that's me,' said the old fellow, and touched his cap. 'How do you know my name?'

'Well, Jackson, the taxi driver, told us he was your great-grandson,' said Julian. 'You see we're staying at the old lighthouse – and Jackson said you could tell us a few things about it – its history, you know. And about the wreckers that lived here before the lighthouse was built.'

'Oh, I can tell you tales all right!' said Jeremiah, puffing out a cloud of smoke, and making Mischief cough. 'That's more than that silly young great-grandson of mine can! He don't know nothing, nothing at all – except about cars. Well, who wants cars, nasty, smelly noisy things? Pah! That young George Jackson is a ninny!'

'He's not. He's the cleverest mechanic in the place!' said George, at once. 'There's not a thing he doesn't know about cars!'

'CARS! There now, what did I say – nasty, noisy, smelly things!' said Jackson's great-grandad, with a snort.

'Well, look – we don't want to talk about cars,' said Julian. 'You tell us about the old days – the wreckers and all that!'

'Ah – the old days!' said Great-Grandad. 'Well, I knew some wreckers myself, once – there was One-Ear Bill, now . . .' And then old Jeremiah told a story that the Five could hardly believe!

CHAPTER TWELVE

Jeremiah's tale

'Now WHEN I was a boy,' began the old man, 'a boy not much older than this here youngster,' and he poked Tinker with his horny forefinger, 'there wasn't a lighthouse out there – but there were always those wicked rocks! And many's the time in a stormy season when ships have been caught by their teeth, a-glittering there, waiting. You know what they're called, don't you?'

'Yes. Demon's Rocks,' said Tinker.

'Well, up on that high cliff there, lived a wicked old man,' said Jeremiah. 'And he had a son as bad as himself, and a nephew too. The Three Wreckers, they was called, and I'll tell you how they came by their name.'

'Did you know them?' asked Dick.

'That I did! And if I was hidden behind a bush when they came marching by, I'd send a stone skedaddling after them!' said the old man. 'Mean and cruel and wicked they were. And everyone was scared of them, right down afraid! There was One-Ear, the old man. They say his left ear was chewed off by a monkey, but do I blame that monkey? No, I do not, not more than I'd blame *your* monkey for chewing off the ear of somebody else I know – but I won't mention no names, he might hear me.'

The old fellow looked over his shoulder as if the man he was thinking of might be about.

'Well – there was One-Ear, the old man – and there was Nosey, the son – and Bart, his nephew – and not a pin to choose between them for meanness. There was only one thing they was after – and that was money! And a mighty wicked way they chose to get it.' The old man stopped and spat in disgust on the pavement.

'Pah! I'll tell you how they got rich, oh yes, I'll tell you. And I'll tell you what happened to them in the end too. Be a lesson to you and to everyone! Well now, you see that high cliff away down the coast there – the one with the flag-post and the flag a-waving in the wind?'

'Yes,' said everyone, looking at the waving flag.

'Now ships mustn't hug the coast beyond that point!' said Great-Grandad. 'If they do, they'll be forced inland by the current, and thrown on those rocks down there – Demon's Rocks. And that's the end of them. No ship has ever been able to escape the sharp teeth of those wicked rocks, once she's caught in that current. Well now, to stop the ships going near to the cliff in those days, they flew a flag in the daytime – and lit a lamp up there at night. And both said as plain as could be "BEWARE! KEEP OUT! DANGER".

'Of course, all sailors knew the flag and the lamp too, and many a one blessed them, and took their ships out to sea, away from Demon's Rocks. But that didn't suit old One-Ear Bill. *He* didn't mind a wreck or two! He'd be down on the beach picking up what he could, if a ship came smashing down on the rocks. And would he save a single soul – not he! There were some people who said he was the Demon of Demon's Rocks himself!'

'What a wicked old man!' said Anne horrified.

'Aye, you're right, missie,' said the old fellow. 'Well, the wrecks didn't come often enough for him and Nosey and Bart. So they put their ugly heads together and thought up as wicked a plan as any man could think of!'

'What was it?' said Tinker, his eyes almost falling out of his head.

'Well, on a stormy night he put out the lamp shining brightly on the far cliff, and he and Nosey carried it to that bit of cliff over there, see?' and the old man pointed to a jutting-out piece nearby. 'And you know what's just below *that* cliff, don't you – all round the lighthouse!'

'Rocks! Sharp, horrible rocks – the Demon's Rocks!' said George, horrified.

'Do you mean to say that One-Ear Bill and the others deliberately shone the lamp there on stormy nights, to guide ships straight on to the rocks?' said Julian.

'Aye, that's exactly what I mean,' said Jeremiah Boogle. 'And what's more I met old One-Ear Bill myself one dark night when the storms were on – and what was he carrying between himself and Nosey – the lamp! They'd doused the light, of course, but I'd my own little lantern with me, and I saw the lamp plain enough. Aye, that I did! And when they saw me, they set Bart on to me, to push me over the cliff, so I wouldn't tell on them. But I got away, and I DID tell on 'em! Ho, yes, I told all right. And One-Ear Bill went to prison, and serve him right, the wicked man. But he didn't care – and why should he? He was rich! RICH!'

'But how was he rich?' asked Dick.

'Well, young man, the ships that came sailing round this coast in those days, came from far-off countries, and many of them carried treasure,' said Jeremiah. 'And One-Ear Bill stole so much gold and silver and pearls and other things from the wrecks, that he knew he wouldn't need to do another day's work when he came out of prison. A rich man he would be – he wouldn't even need to wreck a ship again!'

'But why weren't the stolen goods taken from him?' said Julian.

'He'd hidden them!' said the old man. 'Ah he'd hidden them well, too. Not even Nosey his son, nor Bart his nephew, knew where he'd put them. They were sure he'd got everything hidden in one of the caves in the cliff – but search as they might, they never found the treasure! They went to prison too, but they came out long before old One-Ear Bill was due out – and how they hunted for the gold and silver, and all that One-Ear had hidden away!'

'Did One-Ear Bill get it when he came out of prison?' asked Dick, thinking this was a much more exciting story than he had ever read in a book – and a true one too!

'No. No, he didn't get it,' said Jeremiah, puffing out a cloud of smoke. 'And glad I am to say that. He died in prison, the wicked old man.'

'Well then – what happened to the treasure from the wrecked ships?' asked George. 'Who found it?'

'No one,' said the old man. 'No one at all! It's still there, hidden wherever that old rascal put it. His secret went with him. Bart looked for it, and Nosey too – ho, I've seen 'em in those caves day after day, and with a lamp night after night. But they never found even a pearl necklace. Ho – that was a good joke, that was! They're dead and gone now – but there're relatives of theirs still living in Demon's Rocks, who could do with a bit of that treasure – poor as church mice they are, with two children as skinny as ever you'd see!'

'Doesn't anyone even have an *idea* where the loot from the wrecked ships is?' asked Julian. 'What about the cave we've been hearing about – the Wreckers' Cave?'

'Oh aye – we've a Wreckers' Cave, all right,' said the old man, knocking out his pipe. 'And I reckon about five thousand people have been in it, scouting round, looking into holes and corners hoping to find what Bart and Nosey never did find! Or maybe ten thousand, who knows? I don't mind telling you, I've been there meself – but not a smell of a little gold coin did I ever see! I'll take you there myself some day if you like. But mind – don't you hope to find anything. It's my belief that One-Ear Bill never did hide his treasure there – he just said it was there to fool Nosey and Bart!'

'We'd love to go and see the cave,' said Dick, and George nodded her head in delight. 'Not to hunt for treasure, of course – it's pretty obvious it's not there now – maybe somebody *did* find it, and took it away secretly!'

'Maybe,' said Jeremiah. 'All right, young man – you come and tell me when you're ready. I'm sitting here most days. And if you've any nice sweets you don't have any use for, think of me, see?'

'We'll go and buy you some straightaway,' said Julian. He couldn't help laughing. 'What kind do you like?'

'Oh, you tell Tom the sweetshop owner it's for old Jeremiah Boogle – he'll give you what I like,' said the old man. 'And mind now – don't you go snooping round them old caves by yourselves – you might get lost. It's a proper laby – laby . . .'

'Labyrinth,' said Julian, smiling. 'Right – we'll be careful.'

The Five went off, Timmy glad to be on the move again. He couldn't understand the old man's story of course, and he wondered why George hadn't taken him for his usual after-breakfast walk. He gave a little whine, and she patted his big head.

'Sorry, Timmy!' she said. 'That old man told such an interesting story that I quite forgot you were longing for a walk. We'll go for one now.'

'Let's call in at the sweetshop first, shall we?' said Julian. 'That old chap deserves an extra something for his tale. Goodness knows how much was true – but he certainly told it well!'

'Of *course* it was true!' said George. 'Why ever should he tell lies?'

'Well – he might have, to get some sweets, you

know!' said Julian, smiling. 'I don't blame him! It's a jolly good story – but please don't think there's any treasure still hidden somewhere, George. It's no use believing that.'

'Well, I do believe it!' said George, defiantly. 'I think he was telling the truth, sweets or no sweets. Don't you, Tinker?'

'Oh *yes*,' said Tinker. 'You wait till you see the caves round about here! Hoo – there might be any *amount* of treasure there, and no one would ever know! I did hunt round a bit myself – but those caves are scary, and when I coughed once, my cough came echoing back to me a hundred times and I was so scared I ran for my life – and fell splash into a pool!'

Everyone laughed. 'Let's buck up and do our shopping,' said Dick. 'And then what about going for a good long walk?'

'Well, *I* don't want to carry eggs and bread and milk for miles,' said George. 'I say a walk first – and then we'll come back, have ice-creams, do our shopping – and go back to the lighthouse.'

'Right!' said Julian. 'Come on, Timmy. We're off for a WALK – a WALK! Ha, that's the word to set your tail wagging, isn't it? Look at it, Mischief. Don't you wish you could wag *your* tail like that!'

CHAPTER THIRTEEN

A pleasant morning – and a shock!

'WHERE SHALL we go for our walk?' said George, as they wandered through the village. 'Oh look – there's a tiny little shop with Tom's Sweetshop written over the door. Let's get the sweets while we remember.'

So in went Julian, and rapped on the counter. A very small man, like a hobgoblin, appeared out of a dark corner.

'I want some sweets for Jeremiah Boogle, please,' said Julian. 'I think you know the kind he wants.'

'I do that!' said Tom, scrabbling about on a shelf. 'The amount that old Jeremiah has eaten since I've been here would keep an army going for years. There you are, young man!'

'He tells a fine story,' said Julian, putting down the money for the sweets.

Tom laughed. 'He's been going on about Bart and Nosey and all them old folks, I suppose,' he said. 'He's a funny one, is old Jeremiah. Never forgets a thing, even if it happened eighty or more years ago! Never forgives, either. There're two folk in this village that he spits at when he passes by them. Naughty old man, he is.'

'What have they done to earn his spite?' asked Dick, in surprise.

'Well, they're some kin of his old enemy, One-Ear Bill,' said Tom. 'I reckon he told you about him all right, didn't he?'

'Yes, he did,' said Julian. 'But all that business about the wrecking happened years and years ago! Surely Jeremiah doesn't vent his anger on any descendants of the wicked One-Ear Bill!'

'Oh, but he *does*!' said Tom. 'You see, these two fellows he spits at have the job of showing people round the caves here – especially the Wreckers' Cave – and I reckon old Jeremiah still broods about One-Ear's hidden treasure, and is scared in case these two chaps ever find it. Find it! It's nearly seventy years since all that happened. Why, that lighthouse over there was built over sixty years ago – after that wrecking business went on. No one will come across any treasure now!'

'But surely they *might*,' said George. 'It depends where it was hidden. If it was in some dry, watertight place, it should still be all right. After all, gold and silver don't decay, do they? Wherever it was hidden, it must still be there!'

'That's what all you visitors say!' said Tom. 'And that's what Ebenezer and Jacob say – they're the two chaps who show people round the caves. But they only say that to make a bit of a thrill for the visitors, you know. Same as old Jeremiah does. Takes them in properly! Well – you believe what you like, youngsters – but you won't find any treasure! I reckon the sea took that years ago! Good day to you! I'll give Jeremiah the sweets when he calls in.'

'Well,' said Dick, as soon as they were outside the shop, 'this is all very interesting! I think probably old Tom's right. The reason why the treasure was never found is because it was probably hidden where the sea managed to get at it – in some water-hole, or somewhere like that.'

'I still believe it's somewhere safe,' said George. 'So does Tinker.'

'Oh well . . . I should think probably Timmy believes it as well,' said Dick. 'He has a childlike mind too!'

Dick at once received a hard punch on the back from George. He laughed. 'All right! We'll give you a chance to hunt for the treasure, won't we, Ju? We'll visit the Wreckers' Cave as soon as we can. Let's go up on the cliffs for our walk, and see if we can spot where the first old lamp used to be, that warned ships to swing out to sea, and avoid Demon's Rocks.'

It was a lovely walk along the cliffs. The celandines and tiny dog violets were out, and clumps of pale yellow primroses were everywhere. The breeze blew strongly, and Mischief held tightly to Tinker's right ear, afraid of being blown off his shoulder. Timmy enjoyed himself thoroughly, bounding along, tail flourishing happily, sniffing at everything.

They came to the flag-post set high on the cliff, its great

red flag waving vigorously in the breeze. A notice-board was beside it. George read it.

'This flag warns ships off Demon's Rocks by day. By night the great lighthouse at High Cliffs, farther along the coast, gives warning. In the old days a lamp shone from this spot to give the ships warning, and later a small lighthouse was built out on Demon's Rocks. It is still in existence, but is no longer in use.'

'Ha – they're wrong there!' said Tinker, pointing to the last sentence. '*We're* using it! I'll alter the notice!' and Tinker actually took a pencil to scratch out the last six words!

Julian took it from him. 'Don't be silly. You can't mess about with public notices. Don't say you're one of the idiots who like to scribble all over the place!'

Tinker held out his hand for the pencil. 'All right. It was just that I thought it wanted correcting. I'm *not* the kind of idiot who scribbles on walls or public notices.'

'Right,' said Julian. 'Tinker, can we see Demon's Rocks – the rocks themselves, I mean, with our lighthouse – from these cliffs?'

'No,' said Tinker. 'The cliff swings away to the left, look, and the Demon's Rocks are away right round the corner, if you see what I mean – so no ship should follow the coastline here, but should keep well out at sea, or it'd be on the rocks. You can see quite well that if the wreckers took the lamp from its warning place here, and put it much farther back, along the way we've come, the ships would swing too far inland, and find themselves wrecked!'

A PLEASANT MORNING – AND A SHOCK!

'I think *I* should have hated old One-Ear Bill as much as old Jeremiah does,' said George, imagining the beautiful ships being ground to pieces all those years ago – just because of a greedy man who liked the pickings from wrecks!

'Well, we'd better go back,' said Julian, looking at his watch. 'We've some shopping to do, remember! Better buck up too – it looks like rain all of a sudden!'

He was right. It was pouring by the time they reached the village! They crowded into a little shop that said 'Morning Coffee' and ordered a cup each, and buns. The buns were so nice that they bought some to take back to the lighthouse with them. Then Anne remembered postcards.

'We *must* buy some,' she said, 'and send one off today. Better get some now, and write one and post it while we're here.'

Dick slipped out of the coffee shop and returned with a packet of very gaudily coloured cards. 'Some of them show the lighthouse,' he said. 'We'll send one of those – and you choose a card to send to your father too, Tinker.'

'It would be a waste,' said Tinker. 'He wouldn't even bother to read it.'

'Well, send one to your mother,' said Anne.

'I haven't one,' said Tinker. 'She's dead. She died when I was born. That's why my father and I always go about together.'

'I'm very, very sorry, Tinker,' said Anne, shocked. The others were sorry too. No wonder Tinker was so wild. No mother to teach him anything! Poor Tinker! Anne felt as if she wanted to buy him every bun in the shop!

'Have another bun, Tinker,' she said. 'Or an ice-cream. I'll pay. Mischief can have one too.'

'We're *all* going to have another bun each, *and* an ice-cream,' said Julian. 'Timmy and Mischief too. Then we'll do our shopping and go home – home to the lighthouse. That sounds grand, doesn't it!'

They wrote three cards – one to Uncle Quentin and Aunt Fanny – one to Joanna – and one to the professor. 'Now they'll know we are safe and happy!' said Anne, sticking on the stamps.

The rain had stopped, so they went to do their shopping – fresh bread, more butter and eggs, two bottles of milk, some fruit and a few other things. Then off they went down to the little jetty.

'Tide will soon turn,' said Julian, as they jumped down from the jetty to the rocky little beach. 'Come on – we'll just have time to walk over the rocks to the lighthouse. PLEASE don't drop the eggs, Tinker!'

They made their way over the rocks, jumping over little pools here and there and avoiding the slimy strands of seaweed that in places covered the rocks. The lighthouse seemed very tall as they came up to it.

'It's *tiny* compared to the great new one away at High Cliffs,' said Tinker. 'You ought to go over that! The revolving lamp at the top is magnificent! Its light is so powerful that ships can see it for miles!'

'Well, this little lighthouse looks nice enough to me at the moment,' said Dick, climbing up the stone steps to the strong wooden door. 'Hallo! Look – two bottles of milk on the top step! Don't tell me the milkman's been!'

'He used to call when my father and I were here,' said Tinker. 'Only when the tide was out in the morning though, because he hasn't a boat. I suppose he heard *we* were all staying here, and came to see if we wanted milk – and left two bottles when he found we were out. He probably yelled through the letter-box and when we didn't answer he just left the milk, on chance.'

'Sensible fellow!' said Dick. 'Get out your key, Tinker, and unlock the door.'

'I don't remember locking it behind us when we went out this morning,' said Tinker, frantically feeling in all his pockets. 'I must have left it in the lock on the inside of the door. Let's see now – we locked the door last night, and left the key in the lock. So I *must* have unlocked it this morning for us all to get out.'

'That's right – but after you unlocked it you ran straight down the steps with George, and the rest of us followed,' said Julian. 'Anne was last. Did *you* lock the door after you, Anne?'

'No. I never thought of it!' said Anne. 'I just shut the door with a bang and raced after you all! So the key must still be on the other side of the door!'

'Well, if we push the door, it should open!' said Julian, with a grin. 'And the key will be on the inside, waiting for us! Let's go in!'

He pushed hard, for the door shut very tightly – and sure enough, it swung open. Julian put his hand round to the inside lock to feel for the key.

It wasn't there! Julian looked at the others, frowning.

'*Someone's been here* – and found the door unlocked – taken the key – and probably plenty of other things as well!' he said. 'We'd better go and look. Come on!'

'Wait – there's something on the doormat,' said Dick, picking up a letter. 'The postman has visited the lighthouse too – here's a letter forwarded from Kirrin – so at least *two* people came while we were out! But surely neither of them would take the key – or anything else either!'

'Well – we'll soon see!' said Julian, grimly, and up the first bend of the spiral stairway he went, at top speed!

CHAPTER FOURTEEN

The old, old map

JULIAN AND Dick went into each room of the lighthouse, racing up the spiral stairway from one to the other. Why, oh why, hadn't they watched to see that Tinker locked the door and took the key!

Yes – a few things *had* been taken!

'My rug!' said George. 'That's gone!'

'And my purse,' said Anne. 'I left it here on the table. That's been taken, too!'

'So has my little travelling clock,' groaned Julian. 'Why did I bring it? I could have used my watch!'

There were a few other things gone, all small. 'Horrible fellow, whoever he is, to creep into the lighthouse while we were out and take our things!' said Anne, almost crying. 'Who would come here – they would surely be seen from the quay, wouldn't they?'

'Yes – you're right there,' said Julian. 'Though probably the thief slipped in when it was pouring with rain, and the quay was deserted! I think we'll have to tell the police, you know. Let's have our dinner, and then I'll take the boat and slip across to the village. The tide will be in then, and I shan't be able to walk over the rocks. Blow that thief! I was looking forward to a nice quiet read this afternoon!'

After their meal, Julian took the boat and rowed across to the jetty. He went straight to the police station, where a stolid-looking policeman listened to him, and wrote slowly in a book.

'Have you any idea who the thief might be?' asked the policeman. 'Or if anyone came to the lighthouse while you were out?'

'Well, two people seem to have come,' said Julian. 'The milkman, because we were surprised to find milk bottles on the step. And the postman. There was a letter for us on the mat inside the door. I don't know of anyone else.'

'Well, as far as I can tell you, both Willy the Milkman, and Postie are as honest as the day,' said the policeman, scratching his chin with his pencil. 'There may have been a third visitor – one who didn't leave milk or a letter! I'll see if anyone was on the quay this morning, who saw the thief going over the Demon's Rocks. Er – do you suspect anyone?'

'Good gracious, no!' said Julian. 'I don't know anyone here – unless you can count Jeremiah Boogle, or Tom the sweetshop owner!'

'No. No, I think we can rule both of them out,' said the policeman, smiling. 'Well, I'll do what I can, and let you know if I hear of anything. Good afternoon, and by the way, as you can't lock that lighthouse door now, and it's plain there are thieves about, I shouldn't leave the lighthouse empty, see?'

'Yes. Yes, I'd already thought of that,' said Julian. 'I

can jam the door all right with something when we're *in* the lighthouse – but I can't do that when we're out.'

'Well – it looks as if we're in for a wet spell,' said the policeman. 'So maybe it won't be much hardship to keep indoors. I hope you're comfortable in the lighthouse – seems a funny place to stay, really.'

'Oh we're *very* comfortable, Constable,' said Julian, smiling. 'Why not pay us a call sometime, and see us?'

'Thanks,' said the policeman, and took Julian to the door.

The constable was right in forecasting a wet spell. It poured all that afternoon, and the little company in the lighthouse whiled away the time playing cards. Julian and Dick had managed to find a heavy piece of wood in the storeroom to jam the door from the inside. They all felt much safer when they knew that had been done! Now no one could get in without making a terrific noise!

'I'm stiff,' said George, at last. 'I want to stretch my legs. I've a good mind to run up and down the stairway half a dozen times.'

'Well, go on, then,' said Dick. 'Nobody's stopping you!'

'How far down does the lighthouse go, Tinker?' asked George. 'We always scoot up the first bit of the spiral stairway and never think about the lighthouse foundations deep down in the rock. *Are* they deep down?'

'Oh, they are,' said Tinker, looking up from his book. 'My father told me that when the lighthouse was built, they drilled right down into the rock for a long way – made a kind of shaft. And he said that under these rocks there are all kinds of queer holes and tunnels – the drill kept shooting downwards when it came to a sudden space.'

'*Really*?' said Dick interested. 'I hadn't thought of what would have to be done to make a high lighthouse safe from the gales and storms. It would *have* to have deep foundations, of course!'

'My father found an old map somewhere,' said Tinker. 'A sort of plan made when the lighthouse was first built.'

'Like architects draw when they plan how to build a house?' said Anne.

'Something like that,' said Tinker. 'I can't remember much about it. I know it showed all the rooms in the lighthouse, connected by the spiral stairway – and it showed the big lamp-room at the top – and at the bottom of the map the foundation shaft was drawn.'

'Can you go down the shaft?' asked Dick. 'Is there a ladder, or anything?'

'I don't know,' said Tinker. 'I've never been down there. I never thought about it!'

'Do you know where the old map is – the one made by the architect who drew up plans for the lighthouse builder to follow?' said Julian. 'Where did your father put it?'

'Oh, I expect he threw it away,' said Tinker. 'Wait a minute though – it may be in the lamp-room! I remember him taking it up there, because it had a drawing of how the lamp worked.'

'Well, I'd rather like to go and see if I can find it,' said

Julian, interested. 'Come up with me, Tinker. Thank goodness you don't keep turning into some sort of car now – you must be growing up!'

So the two of them went up the spiral stairway to the lamp-room at the very top of the tower. Again Julian marvelled at the magnificent views all around. The rain had stopped for a time, and the sea, swept by strong winds, was a swirling tumult of angry waters.

Tinker scrabbled about in a little dark space under the lamp. He at last brought up a roll of something white and waved it at Julian. 'Here's the map. I thought it would be in the lamp-room.'

Julian took it down to the others, and they spread it out. It showed the plan of the lighthouse, and was very clearly and beautifully drawn.

'How is it that architects draw so marvellously?' said George. 'Are they architects because they can do this kind of thing so well – or do they draw beautifully because they are architects?'

'A bit of both, probably,' said Julian, bending over the finely drawn plan. 'Ah – here are the foundations, look – my goodness, they do go down a long way into the rock!'

'Great tall buildings like this *always* have deep, strong foundations,' said Dick. 'Last term at school we studied how . . .'

'Let's not talk of school,' said Anne. 'It's already looming in the distance! Tinker – can anyone get down into this foundation place?'

107

'I told you – I don't know,' said Tinker. 'Anyway I should think it would be a horrible place down there – dark and smelly, and narrow, and . . .'

'Let's go and see,' said George, getting up. 'I'm so bored at the moment that if I don't do something, I'll fall asleep for a hundred years.'

'Idiot,' said Dick. 'Still – quite a good idea of yours. We'd have a bit of peace and quiet while you were sleeping! Oooooch – don't jab me like that, George!'

'Come on,' said George. 'Let's trot down and find out what's down the shaft.'

Anne didn't want to go down the shaft, but the others ran down the stairway, Timmy too, and soon came to the bottom, opposite the entrance door of the light-house.

Tinker showed them a large, round trap-door in the floor there. 'If we open that, we'll be looking down into the foundation shaft,' he said.

So they pulled up the large, round, wooden trap-door, and gazed downwards. They could see nothing at all except darkness! 'Where's my torch?' said Julian. 'I'll fetch it!'

Soon his torch was lighting up the round shaft, and they saw an iron ladder going down it on one side. Julian climbed down a few steps and examined the walls of the shaft.

'They're cement!' he called. 'And they must be enormously thick, I should think. I'm going on down.'

So down he went, and down, marvelling at the sturdy cement lining of the enormous shaft. He wondered why it had not been filled in. Perhaps a hollow cement-lined shaft was stronger than a filled-in one? He didn't know.

He came almost to the bottom – but he didn't go down the last steps of the iron ladder. A peculiar noise came from below him! A gurgling, choking noise! What in the world could it be?

He shone his torch down to see – and then stared in amazement! There was water at the bottom of the shaft, water that swirled and moved around, making a strange, hollow, gurgling noise. Where did it come from?

As he watched it, it disappeared – then it came back again! He shone his torch here and there to find out how the water made its way into the shaft.

There must be a tunnel or a passage of some sort down there, that the sea can enter, he thought. It's high tide now – so the water is swirling in. I wonder – now I *wonder* – if it's free of water when the tide is out! And if so where does that tunnel, or whatever it is, lead to? Or is it always under water? I'll go back and tell the others – and have another look at that old map!

He climbed back, glad to be out of the smelly darkness of the old shaft. The others were at the top, looking down rather anxiously.

'Here he is!' said George. 'See anything interesting, Julian?'

'I did, rather,' said Julian, climbing out of the shaft. 'Got that old map with you? I want to look at something, if so.'

'Come upstairs, then,' said Dick. 'We can see better there. What was down there, Ju?'

'Wait till we're up in the living room,' said Julian. He took the map from Tinker as soon as he arrived there, and sat down to look at it. He ran his finger down the shaft to the bottom, and then jabbed at a round mark drawn there.

'See that? That's a hole at the bottom of the shaft, through which sea-water comes in. It's high tide now, so the water is seeping into the shaft – but it's not very deep. At low tide there wouldn't be a single drop coming in. Wouldn't I love to know where that water-tunnel went to – up to the surface of the rocks? Through them to some-where a good way off? Or what?'

'An undersea tunnel!' said George, her eyes bright. 'Why don't we explore it sometime when the tide is out?'

'Well – we'd have to be pretty certain we wouldn't suddenly be drowned!' said Julian, rolling up the map. 'Very interesting, isn't it? I suppose the hole was left in case the constant push of water there, when the tide was in, might undermine the foundations. Better to have the shaft half-full of water than eaten away by constant tides!'

'Well,' began Anne, and then suddenly stopped in fright. A very loud voice came up the stairway, and made everyone jump violently.

'ANYONE AT HOME? HEY, ANYONE AT HOME?'

CHAPTER FIFTEEN

Jacob is in trouble

'WHO'S THAT shouting like that?' said Anne, fearfully. 'It can't be the robber, can it?'

'Of course not,' said Julian, and went to the door of the living room. He yelled down the stairway:

'Who is it? What do you want?'

'It's the police!' shouted back the enormous voice.

'Oh. Come on up, then,' said Julian, relieved. Footsteps could be heard coming up the iron stairway, accompanied by loud puffs and pants. Then a policeman's helmet appeared, followed by his shoulders and the rest of him. Soon he was standing in the living room, beaming round at the surprised company, panting with the effort of climbing so many stairs.

'How did you get in?' asked George. 'We jammed the door shut from the inside.'

'Well, I managed to unjam it, miss,' said the policeman, mopping his forehead, and smiling. He was the same policeman that Julian had seen that afternoon. 'Not much protection that, really. You ought to get a new key made.'

'How did you get over here – the tide's in,' said Julian. 'You couldn't have walked over Demon's Rocks.'

'No. I got Jem Hardy's boat,' said the policeman. 'By the way, my name's Sharp – Police Constable Sharp.'

'A very good name for a policeman,' said Julian, with a cheerful grin. 'Well, have you caught the thief who took our key, and the other things?'

'No. But I've a pretty good idea who it is,' said Sharp. 'I couldn't find anyone who'd been sitting on the quay during the time you were away from the lighthouse, but I did by chance find a lady whose windows look down on the jetty, and she happened to see someone standing about there. She said he went over the rocks to the lighthouse.'

'Who was it? The milkman, the postman?' asked Dick.

'Oh no, I told your friend they were good fellows,' said the constable, looking quite shocked. 'It was er – well, a man who's a bit of a bad lot.'

'Who's that?' asked Julian, suddenly afraid it might be old Jeremiah. *Could* he be a bad lot – he had sounded such a good fellow!

'Well, it's no one you know,' said Sharp. 'It's one of a family with rather a bad name – a man called Jacob – Jacob Loomer. He comes of a family that used to do a bit of wrecking, and . . .'

'Wrecking! Old Jeremiah was telling us of long-ago wreckers!' said Dick. 'One was called Nosey – and another was called Bart – relations of a well-known wrecker called One-Ear – er, One-Ear . . .'

'Bill,' said Sharp. 'Ah, yes – One-Ear Bill. He lived a long time ago, when old Jeremiah was a young man. This

114

here Jacob, the one that was seen going into your light-house today, would be his great-great-great grandson, I reckon – something like that. Living image of old One-Ear Bill, according to Jeremiah. There's a bad strain in that family – can't seem to get it out!'

'Well – you say it was Jacob who came into the light-house? Why can't we have him arrested then?' said Julian. 'And make him give up the key he took – and the other things?'

'Well, if you'll come along with me and identify your things, maybe I can do something about it,' said the constable. 'But he may have hidden them all by now – though he's that free-handed I wouldn't be surprised if he hasn't *given* them all away. A bit of a fool, Jacob is, as well as a rogue. Ah – he'd have liked the job of wrecking ships, he would – right up his street.'

'I'll come with you now,' said Julian. 'The others don't need to, do they?'

'Oh no – you'll do,' said the policeman, and he and Julian went down the spiral stairway to the entrance. The others heard the door bang, and looked at one another.

'Well! To think that a great-great-great grandson of that horrid old One-Ear Bill is still living in the same place that the old wrecker himself did!' said Dick. '*And* he's a rogue too. History repeating itself?'

'We *must* go and see the Wreckers' Cave tomorrow, if we can,' said George. 'Jeremiah Boogle said he would show it to us.'

'So long as there isn't an old, old wrecker hiding there!' said Anne. 'Older than Jeremiah Boogle – with a beard down to his feet – a sort of Old Man of the Sea – with a horrid gurgling voice, and eyes like a fish!'

'*Really*, Anne!' said George astonished. 'I'll be scared to go into caves if you say things like that!'

'I wonder how Julian's getting on,' said Tinker. 'Mischief, stop jigging up and down – you make me feel out of breath!'

Julian was at Jacob's house, and there, sure enough, were the things he had stolen – the rug, the clock and Anne's purse – empty now!

'And what about the key?' demanded the constable. 'Come on now, you took the key out of the door of the lighthouse, we know you did. Give it here, Jacob.'

'I didn't take it,' said Jacob, sullenly.

'I'll have to take you in, you know, Jacob,' said the constable. 'You'll be searched at the police station. Better give up the key now.'

'Search me all you like!' said Jacob. 'You won't find that key on me. I tell you. I didn't take it. What would I want that key for?'

'For the same reason that you usually want keys for,' said the constable. 'For breaking in and stealing. All right, Jacob. If you won't let this young gentleman have his key, I'll have you searched at the police station. Come along with me.'

But alas, no key was found on the surly Jacob, and the constable shrugged his shoulders and raised his eyebrows at Julian.

'If you take my advice, I'd get a different lock put on your door. Jacob's got your key somewhere. He'll be at the lighthouse again as soon as he sees you all go out.'

'Bah!' said Jacob, rudely. 'You and your keys. I tell you I didn't take it. There wasn't a key there . . .'

'Come along with me, Jacob,' said the constable. He turned to Julian. 'Well, that's all. We'll have his house searched. The odds are that he's hidden the key somewhere. He's an artful dodger, this one!'

Julian went back to the lighthouse, rather worried. It

might take a few days, in a little place like this, to have a
new lock put in. In the meantime they would either have to
keep themselves prisoners in the lighthouse – or leave a
front door that anyone could open!

The others listened excitedly to his tale, when he went
back. They were glad to have the rug, the clock and the
purse again – though Anne was sad that all her money was
gone.

'We'll have to get a new lock and key,' said Julian.
'After all, this lighthouse has only been *lent* to us, and it's
our responsibility to look after it and all it contains. It's a
good thing it was only *our* things that were taken – not
Professor Hayling's!'

'It's getting rather late,' said Anne, jumping up. 'We
haven't had our tea yet! I'll get it. Anyone feel like buns
with butter and jam?'

Everyone did, and soon Anne produced a large plate of
delicious-looking buns. They talked as they drank their
tea, and ate the buns.

'I vote we go and find Jeremiah Boogle tomorrow, and
see if he's heard of the robbery, and if he has anything
interesting to say about it,' said George.

'And also we really must get him to show us the
Wreckers' Cave,' said Julian. 'By the way, what were
the names of the two men who have the job of showing
the visitors round the caves? I'm pretty sure one was
Jacob!'

'You're right – it was – and the other man was called

118

Ebenezer!' said Dick. 'Well – let's hope Jacob is locked up, or out of the way somewhere when we go to see the caves. We shall get some black looks from him, if not!'

'Well, we can give him some back!' said George, putting on a terrific scowl, and making Timmy give a sudden whine. She patted him. 'It's all right, Timmy – that scowl wasn't for you!'

'We'd better go to the caves tomorrow morning when the tide will be more or less out,' said Julian. 'And I'd better see if I can find a locksmith here who can give us a new lock and key quickly!'

'Why not slip out now?' said Dick. 'I'll come with you for a bit of fresh air. Want to come, girls?'

'No, I'd like to finish my book,' said Anne, and George said the same. Tinker was playing with Mischief, and he didn't want to come either.

'Well, you and the lighthouse will be safe with Timmy and Mischief to look after you!' said Julian, and down the stairway he went, with Dick close behind him.

The locksmith promised to come and look at the door in the next day or two. 'Can't leave my shop just now,' he said. 'Nobody to see to it! It'll take me a few days to do the job for you, I'm afraid.'

'Oh, blow!' said Julian. 'We've already had a thief in the lighthouse! We don't like to go out and leave it empty now!'

They rowed back to the lighthouse, shut and jammed the door as best they could, and went up to the girls.

Timmy gave them an uproarious welcome, and Mischief took a flying leap from a chair back on to Dick's shoulder.

'No lock or key for a few days,' said Dick, sitting down and tickling the delighted little monkey. 'I did want to go and see the caves tomorrow – especially the famous Wreckers' one – but we can't possibly leave the lighthouse empty.'

'Woof,' said Timmy at once.

'He says, why not leave *him* behind, and let him guard it,' said George, solemnly, and Timmy at once said, 'Woof', again.

They all laughed. Dick patted Timmy, and ruffled the fur behind his ears. 'Dear old Tim – all right, *you* guard the lighthouse – you shall have a Very Special Bone for a reward!'

'That's settled then. We leave Timmy here on guard, and we all go off to the caves,' said Julian. 'Well, one of the brothers who show visitors round will be missing tomorrow, I fear – Jacob will *not* be there!'

'I bet we'll get some scowls from the other brother – what's his name now – Ebenezer?' said Anne. 'We'll have to be careful that we don't get pushed into a deep pool of water!'

'Dear me, yes,' said Julian. 'One never knows! We'll certainly be on our guard!'

CHAPTER SIXTEEN

Down in the caves

NEXT MORNING George awoke with a jump. Timmy was pushing her gently with his nose. 'What is it, Tim?' said George. Timmy gave a bark, and ran to where the spiral stairway led downwards.

'Go down and tell the boys what it is you want,' said George, sleepily. So down the stairway went Timmy, and into the room where the boys were sleeping. He trotted in

and nudged Julian with his nose, but Julian was so fast asleep that he didn't stir.

Timmy pawed at him, and Julian awoke with a jump. He sat up. 'Oh, it's you, Tim – what on earth do you want? Is anything wrong with the girls?'

'Woof,' said Timmy, and ran to the spiral stairway. He disappeared down it, barking.

'Blow! He's heard someone!' said Julian, yawning. 'Well, if it's Ebenezer or Jacob – no, it can't be Jacob, of course – I'll tell him what I think of people who steal!'

He unjammed the door of the lighthouse and opened it. On the step stood two milk bottles! 'Well, really, Timmy, fancy waking me because the milkman came!' said Julian, taking in the bottles. 'Good old milkman – I wonder if he had to come by boat – the sea's pretty high this morning – but I suppose he *could* just about have waded over the rocks!'

At breakfast the Five remembered that they meant to see the caves that morning. They had a very fine meal of fried bacon, bought the day before, and eggs, with buttered toast and marmalade to follow. Anne had made some good hot coffee, and they all enjoyed themselves immensely. Mischief made himself a real nuisance by putting a paw deep in the marmalade jar and then, when smacked, running all over the place leaving sticky marmaladey marks everywhere!

'We'd better all take a wet rag with us as we go about the room,' said Anne, in disgust. 'He's run over the table and desk and everything. BAD Mischief! I do so hate feeling sticky.'

Mischief was sad to feel himself in disgrace, and leapt on to Tinker's shoulder, putting his sticky paws lovingly round the boy's neck. 'That's right!' said Tinker, 'rub all your stickiness off on *me*, you little monkey!'

'We'll wash up in the sink, and you boys can tidy up the rooms,' said Anne. 'Then we'll all go out. It's a lovely day.'

'Looks a bit stormy to me,' said Dick. 'What do *you* say, Tim?'

Tim agreed. He thumped his tail vigorously on the floor, making Mischief pounce on it in joy. Anne gathered up the crockery and took it to the sink.

In an hour or so they were ready to go out. 'Let's write a card to Aunt Fanny before we leave,' said Anne. 'Then *that* will be done. We won't say a word about the things that were stolen, though. She might feel upset, and tell us to go back! And *then* what would Uncle Quentin and Professor Hayling say?'

'I bet they're having a wonderful time, arguing all day long, working out figures, and studying papers!' said Julian. 'And I'm pretty certain that Aunt Fanny will have to call them to a meal at least twenty times before they arrive at the table!'

Anne wrote the postcard and put on a stamp. 'Now I'm ready,' she said, standing up. Timmy ran to the top of the stairs, glad that everyone seemed to be on the move at last. He did so love a walk.

'Darling Timmy,' said George, 'I'm afraid you'll have to be left behind to guard the lighthouse! You see, we haven't a key – and we can't jam the door from outside. So please, Timmy dear, stay behind – on guard. You know what *that* means, don't you? ON GUARD!'

Timmy's tail went right down. He gave a small whine. He did so hate being left out of anything – especially a walk. He pawed gently at George as if to say, 'Do please change your mind.'

'On guard, Timmy, now,' said George. 'The lighthouse is in your charge. Don't let ANYONE *in*. You'd better lie on the mat just inside the entrance.'

Timmy ran slowly down behind Julian and the others, looking very mournful indeed. 'Now lie there,' said George, and gave him a pat on the head. 'We'll take you out again soon, and then one of *us* will stay to guard the lighthouse – but this time we *all* want to go out. ON GUARD!'

Timmy lay down on the mat, and put his head on his paws, his brown eyes looking up at George. 'Dear old faithful,' she said ruffling the hair on his head. 'We won't be very long!'

They slammed the door and went down the lighthouse steps. The tide was still out far enough for them to be able to wade over the rocks to the jetty. 'We must be back before it's well in,' said Julian. 'Or we'll have to stay ashore till it's out again. Our boat is tied to the lighthouse post, remember!'

DOWN IN THE CAVES

They went for a stroll along the quay and who should be there, sitting on a stone seat, but old Jeremiah Boogle, smoking his long pipe, staring solemnly out to sea.

'Good morning, Jeremiah,' said Dick, politely. 'I hope we bought the right kind of sweets for you from Tom.'

'Oh aye,' said Jeremiah, puffing out very strong-smelling smoke. 'Hallo, little monkey – so you've come to my shoulder again, have you? Well, what's the news from Monkey Lane?'

The others laughed as Mischief at once poured out a stream of monkey chatter into the old man's ear. 'We thought we would go and see the caves today,' said Julian. 'Especially the old Wreckers' Cave.'

'Now don't you let that Ebenezer take you round!' said the old man, at once. 'You won't find Jacob there – oho – I know what's happened to *him*. And serve him right. Never could keep his fingers to himself, that one! Ebenezer's as bad. He could steal the buttons off your coat, and you'd never know! Now look – what about *me* showing you the caves? I know them inside out, and I can show you things that that rat of an Ebenezer doesn't even know of.'

'Well – we'd certainly much rather *you* took us, and not Ebenezer,' said Julian. 'Ebenezer may be feeling rather angry because we told the police about his brother stealing things. We'll give you some more sweets if *you'll* guide us round.'

'Well, let's go now,' said Jeremiah, getting up very spryly. 'This way!'

And off they went, Mischief too – the little monkey did Jeremiah the honour of sitting on his shoulder all the way down the village street. The old man was delighted to see how everyone stared and laughed.

He took them round the foot of some very high cliffs. They came to a rocky beach farther along, and walked over it. 'There's the entrance,' said the old man, pointing to a large hole in the cliff nearby. 'That's the way to the caves. Got a torch?'

'Yes – we brought one each,' said Julian, patting his pocket. 'Do we have to pay to go in?'

'No. People give Ebenezer a tip – fifty pence or so – if he shows them round – or Jacob, when he's there,' said Jeremiah. *'I'll* deal with Ebby, though. Don't you waste your money on that scoundrel!'

The hole in the cliff led to the first cave, which was a big one. Lighted lanterns hung here and there, but gave very little light.

'Mind your step, now,' warned Jeremiah. 'It's really slippery in places. This way – through this old arch.'

It was cold and damp in the cave, and the children had to go carefully, and avoid the puddles left by the sea. Then suddenly Jeremiah turned a corner and went in a completely different direction! Down and down and down they went!

'Hey – we're going towards the *sea* now surely?' said Julian, in surprise. 'Do the caves go *under* the sea, then? Not away back into the cliff?'

'That's right,' said Jeremiah. 'This is a real rocky coast –

126

and the way we're taking leads down a tunnel under the rocks, and then into the caves deep underground. See the rocky roof over our heads – well, if you listen, you can hear the sea now, mumbling and grumbling over it – that roof is the bed of the sea!'

That was a very strange thought indeed, and rather alarming! Anne gazed fearfully up at the rocky roof overhead, and shone her torch on it, half-expecting to see a few cracks leaking salt water from the sea rolling over the rocky roof! But no – there was a little moisture shining on it, and that was all.

'Are we soon coming to the Wreckers' Cave?' asked George. 'Mischief, stop making those noises. There's nothing to be scared of!'

Mischief didn't like this cold, dark, strange walk under-ground, and had begun to make harsh, frightened noises, and then suddenly gave a loud scared screech.

'Don't! You made me jump!' said Anne. 'Goodness – listen to the monkey's screech echoing all along the tunnel and back! Sounds like a hundred monkeys chattering at once! *Our* voices echo too!'

Mischief was most alarmed to hear the enormous amount of screeches and chattering noises that now filled the tunnel. He began to cry almost like a baby, and clung to Tinker as if he would never let him go.

'I expect he thinks this place is absolutely full of screeching monkeys,' said Anne, sorry for the terrified little creature. 'It's only the echo, Mischief.'

'He'll soon get used to it,' said Tinker, hugging the monkey close to him.

'You want to hear the echo just round the next bend of the tunnel!' said Jeremiah, stroking the little monkey, and very foolishly gave an enormous yell just as they got there!

The yell came back ten times as loud, and the tunnel seemed suddenly full of shouts tumbling over one another. Everyone jumped violently, and Mischief leapt high in the air in terror. He sprang to the ground, and scampered away at top speed, wailing in his little monkey voice. He tore down the tunnel, tail in air, and disappeared round the corner. Tinker was very upset.

'Mischief! Come back!' he yelled. 'You'll get lost!'

And along came the echo at once. 'Get lost, get lost, get lost – lost – lost!'

'Don't you worry about your monkey,' said Jeremiah, comfortingly. 'I've had a score of monkeys in my time – and they always come back!'

'Well, I'll jolly well stay down here till Mischief *does* come back!' said Tinker, in rather a shaky voice.

They came out into a cave. This too was lit by lanterns, though very poorly. They had all heard the murmur of voices as they came to it, and wondered who was there.

Three other visitors were in the cave, sightseeing, like the children. A big burly fellow was with them, with jet-black hair, deep-set dark eyes, and a surly mouth – so like Jacob that Julian guessed at once that he was the brother, Ebenezer.

As soon as Ebenezer set eyes on Jeremiah, he roared in fury.

'You get out! This is *my* job – you get out. *I'll* show the caves to those youngsters!'

And with that such a battle of words followed that the Five were almost deafened, especially as the echo repeated everything very loudly indeed! The three visitors fled away up the tunnel, fearing a fight. Anne was very frightened, and clung to Julian.

Ebenezer came shouting up to old Jeremiah, his hand raised. 'Haven't I told you more than a hundred times to keep out of these caves? Haven't I told you I'M the one to show folks around – and Jacob too?'

'Don't listen to him!' said Jeremiah, turning his back on the angry man. 'He's nothing but a big-mouth, same as his brother Jacob!'

'Look out!' yelled Julian, as the angry Ebenezer rushed at Jeremiah, his fist raised to strike him. 'LOOK OUT!'

CHAPTER SEVENTEEN

Mischief again – and a surprise!

JEREMIAH SAW the angry man coming at him, and very neatly side-stepped. Ebenezer couldn't stop, stepped heavily on a strand of very slippery seaweed – and went sprawling into a corner!

'Ho!' said Jeremiah, delighted. 'Very nice, Ebenezer! Get up, and run at me again!'

'He'd better not,' said Julian, in his most grown-up

voice. 'I shall report him to the police if he does – and that will make a pair of them in two days. Jacob got into trouble yesterday – and now it will be Ebenezer.'

Ebenezer got up, scowling, and glared at Jeremiah, who grinned back in delight. 'Coming at me again, Ebby?' he said. 'It's grand fun to hit an old man, isn't it?'

But Ebenezer was very much afraid that Julian would do what he had threatened, and report him to the police. He rubbed his shoulder where it had struck a piece of rock, and debated what to do.

'Come along,' said Jeremiah, to the five watching children. 'I'll take you down to the Wreckers' Cave. Ebby can come too, if he can behave himself. But maybe he'd like to run away home, and get his shoulder looked to!'

That was enough for Ebby! He was determined to follow the little company, and made rude remarks all the time. So he tailed them, and shouted at them from a safe distance. How they wished they had Timmy with them! He would have made short work of the rude Ebenezer!

'Don't take any notice of him,' said Julian. 'Lead on, Jeremiah. My word, isn't it dark in this tunnel! Good thing we all brought good torches!'

The tunnel came to an end at last and opened out into an extraordinary cave. The roof was unexpectedly high, and the irregular sides were ridged with shelves of rocks. On the shelves were dirty old boxes, a crate or two and some sacks.

MISCHIEF AGAIN – AND A SURPRISE!

'What in the world are those?' asked Dick, shining his torch on them.

'Well young sir, they're just what they look like – ordinary boxes and sacks,' said Jeremiah. 'Put there by Ebenezer and Jacob to fool people! They tells everybody they're what the old wreckers got out of ships they wrecked, years ago! Hoo-hoo-hoo! Anybody that believes those lies *deserves* to be fooled. They're all from Ebby's backyard. Seen them lying there myself! Hoo-hoo-hoo!'

His hoo-hooing laugh echoed round the cave, and Ebenezer made an angry growling noise rather like a dog.

'*I'm* not going to fool these kids,' said Jeremiah. 'You and your sacks and boxes! I know where the old things are, the real old things – oh yes I do!'

'They're no better than the sacks and boxes there, wherever they are!' said Ebby, in a growling voice. 'You're lying, old Jeremiah – you don't know nothing!'

'Take us on farther,' said Dick. 'There must be more caves. I think this is exciting. Is this really where the old wreckers hid the things they salvaged from the wrecks they caused – or just a tale?'

'Oh, this is their cave, that's true enough. Dressed up a bit by Ebby there!' said Jeremiah. 'But *I* know the caves farther on. Ebby doesn't! He's too scared to go farther under the sea. Aren't you, Ebby?'

Ebby said something that sounded rude. Julian turned to Jeremiah eagerly. 'Oh, do take us farther – if it isn't dangerous!'

133

'Well, *I'm* going farther on, anyway,' said Tinker suddenly. 'Mischief hasn't come back – so he must be lost – and *I'm* going to find him!'

Julian saw that Tinker was quite determined. 'Right,' he said. 'We'll come with you. Jeremiah, lead the way! But it's not *really* dangerous, is it? I mean – we don't want to find the sea sweeping through these caves, right up to where we are!'

'Tide's not on the turn yet,' said Jeremiah. 'We're all right for a while. When it comes in, it swirls up this passage here – but it stops at the Wreckers' Cave – that's just too high for it, see? The tunnel runs downwards fast now. It goes right under your lighthouse, have you seen it down at the bottom of the shaft?'

'Good gracious, yes!' said Julian, remembering. 'I went down it – and the sea was swirling in and out at openings in the bottom of the shaft. Do you mean to say that the sea that rises in the shaft at high tide comes racing up into these tunnels too?'

'Aye, that it does,' said Jeremiah. 'You can get from here to the lighthouse under the rocky seabed right to that foundation shaft. But nobody dares! Tide comes in so quickly, you might get caught and drowned!'

Ebby at once shouted something rude again – it sounded as if he was telling Jeremiah to go and get drowned too!

'Do let's go on farther,' said Dick. 'Come on, Jeremiah.'

So Jeremiah led them farther on under the rocky bed of

the sea. It was strange and rather frightening to hear the
constant noise of the water racing over the roof of the
winding tunnel. Their torches lit up slimy walls, and rocky
shelves and hollows.

'You know – this would have been a very good place to
hide treasure,' said Julian, glancing up at a dark hollow in
the roof of the tunnel. 'Though I don't know how anyone
would set about looking for it – there are hundreds of
nooks and crannies – and isn't it *cold* in this tunnel!'

'Well, the sun's rays never penetrate down *here*,' said
Dick. 'My word, the sea sounds pretty loud now!'

'I wish we could find Mischief,' said Anne to George.
'Look at poor Tinker. He's crying. He's pretending not to,
but I could see the tears rolling down his cheeks last time I
flashed my torch on him.'

They stopped to look at something – a strange jelly-like
thing, like an enormous sea anemone. Ebby caught them
up, and bumped into Dick. He rounded on Ebby at once.

'Keep off! Follow us if you like, but don't come so near.
We don't like you!'

Ebby took no notice but kept as close behind everyone
as he possibly could, and Dick realised that he was
probably feeling very scared! Then, as they rounded
another corner of the tunnel, and saw yet another cave,
Tinker gave a yell that echoed everywhere.

'MISCHIEF! LOOK! THERE HE IS! MISCHIEF!'

And sure enough, there was the little monkey, crouched
under a small shelf of rock, shivering in fright. He

wouldn't even go running to Tinker. Tinker had to pick him up and hug him.

'Mischief! Poor Mischief – were you very frightened?' he said. 'You're trembling all over! You shouldn't have run away! You might have been lost for ever!'

Mischief had something clutched in his tiny paw. He chattered to Tinker, and put his furry little arms round his neck. As he did so, he opened one paw – and something fell out and rolled over the rocky floor.

'What have you dropped, Mischief?' said Dick, and shone his torch down on to the floor of the cave. Something was glittering there – something round and yellow! Everyone stared, and a shock of excitement went through Julian, who was nearest. 'A gold coin!' he cried, and picked it up. 'As bright as when it was minted. Mischief, where did you get it from? Look, Dick, look George – it's gold all right!'

Immediately everyone was full of the greatest excitement, one thought only in their heads.

The treasure! Mischief must have found the treasure! It was an old coin – very old. Where *could* Mischief have found it?

'Oh, let's go farther on and see!' cried Dick. 'Jeremiah, it *must* be the treasure! Mischief will lead us to it!'

But Mischief would do nothing of the sort. He was NOT going to lose himself again. He was going to sit on Tinker's shoulders, with an arm safely round the boy's neck! He hadn't liked being lost, all by himself in the dark.

Jeremiah would not go any farther, either. He shook his head. 'No – not today. Tide will soon be sweeping up these tunnels – faster than we can walk. Better turn back now, in case we're caught. Many's the visitor that's had to run for his life, when the tide came up all of a sudden!'

George's sharp ears caught the sound of a 'swooshs-woosh'! Somewhere the tide had crept in! 'Come on!' she said. 'We'd better do what Jeremiah says. The sea's coming up the tunnel now as well as over it – and soon it will be sweeping up the beach too, and in at the cliff passages. We'll be caught in the middle, and have to stay here for ages!'

'No need for alarm, missy,' said old Jeremiah. 'There's a bit of time yet. Halloo – where's Ebenezer gone?'

'Blow – he must have heard us talking about Mischief's gold piece,' said George. 'I forgot all about him! Now he knows that Mischief has found a gold coin, he'll feel sure that the treasure *may* be somewhere down here – and he'll look for it as soon as ever he can! WHY didn't we keep quiet about it?'

'I forgot he was standing near us,' groaned Dick. 'Well I suppose the whole of Demon's Rocks village will know by now that a monkey has found the treasure – and hordes of sightseers will swarm down here, hoping to find it. It must have been put in a pretty dry place, surely, for that coin to be so bright and untarnished.'

'Buck up – we'd better go back as quickly as possible,' said Julian. 'Look at old Jeremiah – he's too thrilled for words! He's planning to find the treasure himself at the earliest possible moment!'

'Well, I vote we have a shot at it ourselves tomorrow,' said Dick, excitement welling up in him at the thought. 'Good old Mischief! You're better than any detective!'

Then away up the tunnels they went, making all kinds of plans. WHAT an excitement!

CHAPTER EIGHTEEN

Back in the lighthouse – and an exciting talk!

OLD JEREMIAH was as excited as the others, but he said very little. He was angry to think that Ebenezer should have been there to see the find. He didn't trust that Ebby – nor that Jacob either! They'd be ferreting after that treasure as sure as nuts were nuts, and monkeys were monkeys! Ha – wouldn't they like to know where it was! He stumped on, up the old tunnels, thinking hard, and at last they came out into the welcome daylight again!

'Here, Jeremiah – buy yourself some more sweets,' said Julian, putting some money into the old man's hand. 'And don't count too much on that treasure! I expect it's just an odd coin that Mischief found in a dry corner somewhere!'

'Thank you!' said the old man. 'I don't want the treasure myself – I'm just hoping that Ebby and Jacob don't find it. They'll be hunting all the time for it now!'

They were glad to be out in the open again. The sun had gone now, and the wind had whipped up. It was raining hard.

'I say – we'd better buck up, else we shan't be able to walk back to the lighthouse over the rocks!' said Julian, worried. But fortunately the wind was against the tide and they just had time to wade over to the lighthouse steps.

'There's our little boat bobbing about,' said Tinker. 'And listen – I can hear old Timmy barking! He's heard us coming!'

So he had. He had been lying on the doormat, his ears glued to the crack under the door, listening. Nobody had come near the lighthouse and not a sound did old Timmy hear but the wind and the sea, and a few gulls gliding by.

'We're back, Timmy!' yelled George, and she pushed at the door. It opened, and Timmy leapt out, almost knocking her over. Mischief sprang on to the dog's back, and chattered at him without stopping.

'He's telling him about the gold coin he found,' said Tinker, with a laugh. 'Oh, I WISH you'd been with us, Timmy. It was grand!'

'It feels as if we've been away for ages,' said George. 'But it wasn't very late after all – unless my watch is slow! I'm hungry. Let's have something to eat and talk about everything – and what we're going to do!'

So, over biscuits and sandwiches and coffee, they talked and talked. 'We must get down to the caves again as soon as possible!' said George. 'I'm absolutely certain that Jacob and Ebby will be down there, hunting for coins, as soon as the tide's out again.'

'Well, we can't do anything today, that's certain,' said Dick. 'For one thing the tide's in now – and for another thing it's blowing up for a storm. Just *listen* to the wind!'

Timmy was sitting as close to George as he possibly could. He hadn't liked her going out without him. She sat

141

with her arm round him, eating her biscuits, occasionally giving him half of one. Tinker was doing the same with Mischief!

The children talked and talked. Where could Mischief have found that coin? Was it one on its own, that the sea had swept into the tunnel? Or was it part of a whole lot of coins? Had it come from an iron-bound box whose wooden sides had rotted away? They talked endlessly, their eyes bright, the round gold coin on the table in front of them.

'I suppose it would be treasure trove if we found it?' said Dick. 'I mean – it would be so old that it would belong to the Crown, and not to anyone in particular.'

'I expect we'd be allowed to keep a few coins ourselves,' said George. 'If only we could go straight away now and hunt in that tunnel! I feel as if I can't wait!'

'Woof,' said Timmy, agreeing though he really hadn't much idea of what they were talking about!

'I say – LISTEN to the sea crashing over the rocks between us and the jetty!' said Julian, startled at the sudden booming. 'The wind must be working up to a gale!'

'Well, bad weather's been forecast for some time,' said Dick gloomily. 'Blow! It'll be jolly difficult rowing to and fro in that little *Bob-About* boat. I doubt if we'd be able to walk across the rocks, even at low tide, with a big sea running before the wind.'

'Oh, don't be so gloomy!' said Anne.

'Well, do you want us to be prisoners here in the lighthouse?' demanded Dick.

'It wouldn't matter – there's plenty of food,' said Anne.

'No there isn't! Remember there are five of us – and Timmy and Mischief as well,' said Dick.

'Shut up, Dick,' said Julian. 'You're scaring Anne and Tinker. This storm will soon blow over – we'll be able to pop out and do some shopping tomorrow.'

But the storm grew fiercer, and the sky became so dark that Anne lit the lamps. Rain slashed against the lighthouse, and the wind made a loud howling noise that made Timmy growl deep down in his throat.

Anne went to look out of the window. She felt frightened when she saw the great waves that came surging over the rocks below. Some of them broke on the rocks, and the spray flew so high that it spattered the window out of which she was looking! She drew back in alarm.

'Do you know what hit the window then? It was spray from a great wave!'

'Whew!' said Julian, and went to the window himself. What a wonderful sight! The sea was grey now, not blue, and it raced along towards the shore, great waves curling over into white manes, spray flying. Out to sea there were angry waves too, topped with white, which turned into spray as the strong wind caught them. Only a few gulls were out, screaming in excitement, allowing the wind to take them along on their great white wings.

'Well, I certainly wouldn't mind being a gull today,' said Dick. 'It must be a wonderful feeling to ride on a storm – no wonder they are screaming in joy!'

'Ee-oo, Ee-oo, EE-OOO, EE-OOOOO! cried the gulls, sounding like cats mewing in hunger.

'I'm sorry for the ships out in this,' said Julian. 'Goodness – think of the sailing ships in the olden days, caught on this rocky coast in a wind like this – it's almost a hurricane!'

'And think of that wicked old One-Ear Bill, gloating when he saw a ship sailing nearer and nearer the rocks!' said George. 'And even taking the warning lamp out of its place on the cliff, and bringing it near here to make sure that any ship out that night would make straight for the rocks – CRASH!'

'Don't,' said Anne. 'I hate to think of things like that.'

'Let's have a game,' said Julian. 'Where are the cards? Move that lamp a bit closer to the table, Dick. It's getting so jolly dark. Now no more talk of wrecks! Think of something cheerful – tea-sup, for instance – the treasure – and . . .'

'You know, I think it would be quite easy to find the treasure,' said Dick, bringing the lamp close to the table. 'Mischief is a very clever little thing. I'm sure he would remember where he found that coin, and lead us straight to the place.'

'It might have been just an odd coin, dropped by the man who hid the hoard,' said Anne.

'It might – but wherever it was found I think we can safely say that the main hoard wouldn't be very far away,' said Dick.

'Well, if we do go hunting we'll have to go when the tide is well out,' said Julian. 'I don't really fancy scrabbling about in those caves and tunnels under the rocky seabed, when I know that somehow or other when the tide is coming in the water gets *under* the seabed, as well as on it.'

Dick sat frowning, thinking out something. 'Ju,' he said at last, 'you remember the direction we went in, as soon as we were underground this morning? We went leftish all the way, didn't we?'

'Yes, we did,' said Tinker, at once. 'I had my little

compass with me – look – it clips to my wristwatch – and we went sharp west all the time.'

'Towards the lighthouse, that would be,' said Julian, and drew a quick plan. 'See – here's the lighthouse, say – and just here is the entrance into the cliff, where we first went – here's the path we took, curving right back to the sea again, under the rocky beach here it goes – and that's a cave, see, then more tunnel, and caves – the way always curving sharply to the left . . .'

'A bit farther on and we'd have been almost under the lighthouse!' said Dick, in amazement.

'That's right,' said Julian. 'And maybe in the old days, before this lighthouse was built, and ships were sent crashing on the rocks on which it now stands, there was a tunnel down from those lighthouse rocks that joined up with the tunnel we were in this morning – so that the wreckers would find it very easy to stow away anything valuable they found in a wrecked ship, without being seen!'

'Whew! You mean they waited till the ship smashed up, then waded over the rocks, as we do, took what they could find, and disappeared down a tunnel there to hide it!'

'And came out the other end!' said Anne.

George stared at Julian, and her eyes were bright.

'Maybe the tunnel is *still* somewhere in these rocks!' she said. 'Somewhere down at the edge of them, because we know the sea gets into the tunnel. Julian, let's look for it tomorrow. I think you're right. There *may* be a hole in the

146

rocks here somewhere, that drops down into the tunnel we were in.'

Nobody wanted to play a game after that! They felt much too excited. They studied Julian's plan again and again, glad that Tinker's little compass had shown him so clearly that morning that the undersea passages had led due west to the lighthouse rocks.

'Do you suppose that everyone has forgotten the old hole?' said Dick. 'Nobody has told us anything about it, not even Jeremiah. Do you think it may have been blocked up?'

Julian frowned, thinking hard.

'Well, yes – it may have been,' he said. 'It *is* odd that Jeremiah didn't say anything about it. Anyway we'll have a good hunt tomorrow.'

'And if we find it, we'll drop down and hunt for the treasure!' said Tinker, his eyes shining. 'WHAT a shock for Ebenezer and Jacob if we find it first!'

CHAPTER NINETEEN

A nasty shock!

THE STORM blew itself out that evening, and next day was much calmer. The sky still looked angry, and rain fell now and again, but it was possible to get out of the lighthouse door in the morning, and go down the steps on to the rocks.

'Shall we go shopping first – or look for the hole?' said Julian.

'Look for the hole,' said Dick, promptly. 'The wind is still pretty strong, and the storm might blow up again – just look at that angry sky! We wouldn't be able to mess about round the edge of the rocks if the sea gets any rougher.'

They spread out and went cautiously over the great rocks on which the lighthouse was built. At low tide the rocks stood well up, out of the sea. The lighthouse was built on the highest part, and seemed to tower over the searchers as they clambered here and there, seeking for any hole that looked as if it might lead down into some tunnel below.

'Here's a hole!' called Anne, suddenly, and they all clambered over to her in excitement, Timmy too. Julian looked down to where Anne was pointing. 'Yes – it does look a likely one,' he said. 'Big enough to take a man, too. I'll climb down and see.'

He slid down the hole, holding on to projecting pieces of rock as he went. The others watched, thrilled. Timmy barked. He didn't like to see Julian disappearing like this!

But before Julian quite disappeared, he shouted again; 'I'm afraid it's no good! It's come to a sudden end! I'm standing on firm rock, and though I've felt all round with my feet, there's no opening anywhere. It's a dead end!'

What a disappointment! 'Blow!' said Dick, lying down on the rocks and putting his arm down the hole to help Julian to climb up again. 'I had high hopes then! Julian – here's my hand. Do you want any help?'

'Thanks – it is a bit difficult!' said Julian. He climbed up with difficulty, and squeezed out of the hole thankfully. 'I wouldn't like to get *wedged* in here!' he said. 'Especially with the tide coming in!'

'It's beginning to pour with rain again!' said Anne. 'Shall we go shopping now – or wait a bit?'

'Oh, let's wait,' said George. 'I'm cold and wet now. Let's go into the lighthouse and make some hot coffee. WHAT a disappointment! Never mind – we can always go down the tunnels we were in yesterday and search around – maybe Mischief will show us where he found the gold coin!'

They all went into the lighthouse, and once more Julian jammed the door. 'I wish that locksmith would come,' he said. 'If we go down into the caves, we'll have to leave old Timmy behind on guard – and it is such a shame!'

'Woof,' said Timmy, heartily agreeing. They all went upstairs and Anne began to make the coffee. As they were sitting drinking it, Timmy suddenly sprang to his feet with a most blood-curdling growl. Everyone jumped, and Anne spilt her coffee.

'Timmy! What's up?' said George, in alarm. Timmy was standing with his nose towards the closed door of the room, his hackles rising up on his neck. He looked truly fierce!

'What on *earth* is the matter, Tim?' said Julian, going to the door. 'There can't be anyone on the stairway – the entrance door's jammed!'

Timmy raced out of the door as soon as Julian opened it and tore down the spiral stairway at such a speed that he fell, and rolled to the bottom. George gave a terrified scream. 'Timmy! Have you hurt yourself?'

But Timmy leapt to his feet at once, and ran to the entrance door, growling so ferociously that Anne felt really frightened. Julian ran down and went to the door. It was still well and truly jammed.

'Timmy! Maybe it's just the poor milkman, come with some milk again,' he said, and unjammed the door. He took hold of the handle to open it.

It wouldn't open! Julian pulled and tugged, but it was of no use. The door simply would NOT open!

By this time everyone was down beside him. 'Let *me* try,' said Dick. 'The door must just have stuck.'

No – he couldn't open it either! Julian looked gravely round at everyone. 'I'm afraid – very much afraid – that SOMEBODY has locked us in!' he said.

There was a horrified silence. Then George cried out in anger. 'Locked us in! How dare they! Who's done this!'

'Well – I think we can guess,' said Julian. 'It was whoever came and stole our key the other day!'

'Ebenezer – no, Jacob!' cried Dick. 'One of the two, anyway. How DARE they? What are we going to do? We can't get out. Why have they done this – this – silly – *wicked* thing?'

'I'm afraid it's because they think we might go looking for the treasure – and find it,' said Julian, his face grave, 'We felt sure that Mischief might remember where he had found the gold coin – and lead us there – and I'm pretty sure they think the same. So this is their way of making sure *they* have time to find the treasure, before we do!'

'They're wicked, they're wicked!' cried George, taking hold of the handle of the door, and pulling it violently. 'We're prisoners!'

'Don't pull the handle off, old thing,' said Julian. 'That wouldn't help at all. Let's go upstairs and talk about it. We'll have to think of some way out of this unexpected difficulty.'

They went soberly upstairs again, and sat down in the living room. Yes – they were certainly prisoners!

'What are we going to do?' said Dick. 'We are in a real fix, Julian.'

152

A NASTY SHOCK!

'Yes. You're right,' said Julian, looking worried. 'We can't get out of the lighthouse, that's certain. On the other hand – how can we get help? No telephone. Shouting would never be heard. Can't use our boat. No one would ever know we are prisoners – they've seen us going in and out of the lighthouse, and if we suddenly don't appear any more they'll simply think we have gone home, and that the lighthouse is empty again!'

'We shall die of starvation!' said Anne, scared.

'Oh no – I expect we shall think of something,' said Dick, seeing that Anne was really frightened. 'All the same, it's a puzzle. We can't get *out* – and no one can get *in*! Whoever locked that door has certainly taken the key away with him.'

They talked and they talked, and finally they felt hungry, so they had a meal – though they felt that they ought to eat sparingly, in case their food ran short too quickly.

'And I feel so hungry,' complained George. 'I *keep* feeling hungry here.'

'That's what I told you. Living in a lighthouse somehow makes you feel hungry all the time!' said Tinker.

'We'll try and catch the milkman tomorrow morning,' said Julian, suddenly. 'Let's see, now – we could write a note, and push it under the door, so that he would see it tomorrow when he comes. We could put HELP – WE ARE LOCKED IN.'

'It would blow away,' said George. 'You know it would.'

'We could pin it down our side – and then it wouldn't,' said Anne. 'Half of it would still stick out under the door.'

'Well, it's worth trying,' said Dick, and immediately wrote out the note on a large sheet of paper. He shot downstairs to pin it to the mat – and shoved half the paper underneath so that it stuck out on the other side of the door.

He ran back upstairs. 'I don't for a moment think that the milkman will come across the rocks in this weather,' he said. 'They'll be almost impassable. Still we'll hope for the best.'

There didn't seem anything else to do. The evening came early, for the sky was dark again, and the wind once more got up, and howled dismally. Even the gulls decided that it was no longer a good idea to glide to and fro.

They played games that evening, and tried to laugh and make jokes. But secretly everyone was worried. Suppose that the stormy weather went on and on, and nobody guessed they were locked in the lighthouse, and the milkman didn't bring any milk, and didn't see the note – and they ate all their food and . . .

'Cheer up, everyone,' said Julian, seeing the dismal looks around the table. 'We've been in worse fixes than this.'

'Well, *I* don't think we have!' said Anne. 'I just can't see ANY way out of this one!'

There was rather a long silence during which Timmy sighed heavily, as if he too was worrying! Only the monkey seemed cheerful, and went head-over-heels at top speed

round the room, sitting up for laughs at the end. But
nobody laughed. Nobody even seemed to notice him.
Mischief felt very sad, and crept over to Timmy for
comfort.

'There is one idea that *might* be a good one,' said Julian,
at last. 'It's been running round in my head for a while –
and I'm not sure whether it's possible or not. Anyway, it's
one we might try tomorrow, if help doesn't come.'

'What?' asked everyone at once, and Timmy lifted his
head and whined, as if he too quite understood.

'Well, do you remember that I went down that foundation shaft?' said Julian, 'and saw the water swirling at the
bottom? Now – do you suppose it's at all possible that that
shaft was bored down through a *natural* hole – and the
lighthouse builders chose to put the foundation shaft there
because there was a ready-made shaft they could use? – a
fine hole going right down through the rock! And they
made the hole into a cement-lined shaft, strong and
everlasting, so that the lighthouse would never be at the
mercy of the waves and wind – but would stand firm,
whatever happened?'

This was a new idea to everyone, and it took a little
while to sink in. Then Dick smacked the table top and
made them all jump.

'Julian! You've got it! Yes – that strong cement-lined
shaft runs down a *natural* hole – and that hole must be the
one we've been looking for! The one that connects up with
the tunnels we were in yesterday! No wonder we couldn't

find it when we hunted all over the rocks! The shaft-makers used it!'

There was silence again. Everyone was taking this in, even Tinker. Julian looked round the table and smiled. 'Have you all jumped to it?' he said. 'If that *is* the hole we were looking for – what about one of us going down that iron ladder again to the bottom – and finding out if it *does* lead into the tunnel we were in yesterday?'

'And walking through it, and up the passage and coming out through the cliff entrance we used yester-day!' said George. 'Julian! What an absolutely wonderful idea! We could escape that way! What a shock for Ebby and Jacob! We'll do it somehow – we'll DO it!'

CHAPTER TWENTY

Down the shaft and into the tunnel

IT WAS a most exciting idea to think that the iron ladder in the great cement-lined shaft might possibly lead to the tunnel they had been into yesterday. Julian had seen water swirling at the bottom, when the tide was in – possibly if they went down it when the tide was going out, there would be no danger of being trapped!

The storm was very fitful now – sometimes it came back again, and then the wind blew so hard that it seemed as if the buffeted lighthouse must fall! Rain fell in torrents that night, and during the dark early hours of the morning, when the tide was in, great waves pounded over the rocks, sending spray almost over the top of the lighthouse. Julian awoke and looked out of the bedroom window in awe.

'I hope there's no ship out anywhere near here tonight,' he said, and then gave a sudden exclamation. 'What's that – something swept right across the sky!'

'It's the beam from the new lighthouse at High Cliffs, said Dick. 'I saw it last night. It must have a very powerful beam, mustn't it, to show even on a night like this?'

They watched for a little while, and then Julian yawned.

'Let's try to go to sleep,' he said. 'We thought we were

going away for a nice little holiday – and BANG – we're in the middle of something again!'

'Well, let's hope that we come out of it all right,' said Dick, settling down in his rugs once more. 'I must say that I feel a bit cut off from civilisation at the moment. 'Night, Julian.'

In the morning the storm was still about, and the wind was terrific. Julian ran down to the entrance door to see if the milkman could possibly have come – and had seen their message for help.

But no – the paper was still half on their side, flapping on the mat. Obviously the milkman hadn't dared to cross the rocks that morning, either on foot or by boat!

Dick had looked out of the window to make sure that their boat was still safely moored to the post – and to his surprise and distress, it was no longer there! Tinker was very upset.

'Where's my little boat gone? Has somebody stolen it?'

'Maybe – or possibly the storm broke the mooring rope, and the boat was smashed to pieces on the rocks,' said Julian. 'Anyway, it's gone. Poor old Tinker. What a shame!'

Tinker was very sad, and Mischief tried to comfort him, doing all sorts of silly tricks to make him laugh. But Tinker wouldn't laugh. He really was right down in the dumps.

They had rather a sparse breakfast, and were very silent. Anne cleared away and washed up, and then Julian called them all together.

DOWN THE SHAFT AND INTO THE TUNNEL

'Well, now we must decide about this descent down the shaft to what we hope will be the tunnel we were in,' he said. 'I am going down myself.'

'Toss for it!' said Dick, at once. 'There's no reason why *I* shouldn't go, is there? Or what about us both going, in case one gets into trouble, and needs help?'

'Not a bad idea,' said Julian. 'Except that there won't be anyone to look after the girls and Tinker.'

'woof!' said Timmy, indignantly, standing up at once. Julian laughed and patted him.

'It's all right, Timmy. I just wanted to see if you thought *you* could guard them well. All right – Dick and I will go down the shaft. The sooner the better. We simply must go while the tide is out. What about now, Dick?'

Solemnly they all went down the spiral stairway to the entrance door, where the trap was that opened on to the great shaft. Julian pulled up the lid and gazed down into blackness. He shone his torch down, but he could not see the bottom. 'Well – here goes,' he said, and lowered himself down into the shaft, his feet seeking the rungs of the iron ladder. 'Keep cheerful, girls. We'll get through the tunnels and passages, and to the entrance in the cliff – and fetch help for you in no time at all!'

'Julian, please take care,' said Anne, in a shaky voice. 'Please, please do take care!'

Down went Julian, his torch now held between his teeth. After him went Dick. The girls shone their own torches down the shaft, but soon the boys were so far down that they could not be seen. Only their voices came up now and again, sounding very hollow and peculiar.

'We're at the bottom!' shouted Julian, at last. 'It's rock, and there's no water at present! We've a clear way to follow! I crawled out of the hole at the bottom, and there's some kind of tunnel there all right. We're off now – crawling out, and into the tunnel. Cheer up, all of you! See you soon!' And then the peculiar hollow voice stopped, and the girls and Tinker heard nothing more. Timmy began to whine. He couldn't understand these strange goings-on at all!

Julian and Dick were feeling pleased with themselves. It hadn't been very difficult to squeeze out of the arches at the bottom of the shaft. Now they were in a dark narrow tunnel, whose roof sometimes came down so low that they had to bend double. It smelt damp and seaweedy, but there seemed to be plenty of air. In fact at times quite a little breeze seemed to flow round them.

'I shall be glad when we come into a tunnel we recognise!' said Julian, at last. 'We surely must be near where we were yesterday. Hallo, what's this? Dick – look, Dick!'

Dick looked to where Julian's torch was shining and gave a shout. 'A gold coin – another one! We must be near where old Mischief ran off to. Look – there's another – and another. Where on earth did they come from?'

The boys shone their torches all around, and saw at last where the coins had fallen from. Above their heads was a dark hole, running up into the rock. As they shone their torches on it, a gold coin slid out and dropped down to join the others.

'*This* is where Mischief found the coin!' cried Dick. 'Julian there must be a box or something up there which is rotting away, and letting out the money it contains bit by bit.'

'Whoever would have guessed at such a hiding place!' said Julian, marvelling as he shone his torch above his head. 'There's absolutely nothing to be seen except that dark hole – no box, nothing. It must have been pushed right into a recess at the side of the hole, by someone who knew a good hiding place was there.'

'Give me a leg-up so that I can put in my hand and feel,' said Dick. 'Buck up – this is too exciting for words!'

Julian gave him a leg-up, and Dick put his head and shoulders into the hole. He felt to one side – nothing – felt to the other side, and his hand came across something hard and cold – an iron band perhaps? He ran his hand over it and touched something soft and crumbly – old, old wood rotting away, maybe – possibly a wooden chest – only held together by the iron bands. He scrabbled about and Julian gave a sudden shout.

'Hey – you've showered me with money! Whew – I never saw so many gold coins in my life!'

'Julian – I think there's more than one box or chest up there,' said Dick, jumping down, and looking at the big heap of shining coins at his feet. 'There may be a fortune there! Talk about treasure trove! Look – let's not disturb anything else up that hole. No one knows about it except ourselves. Better gather up these coins though, just in *case* that awful Ebby takes it into his head to come down this way!'

So they filled their pockets with the coins and then made their way onwards again. To their joy they soon recognised one of the tunnels they had been in before. 'Plain sailing now,' said Dick joyfully. 'We'll soon be out, and then we'll get the locksmith to pick the lock of the lighthouse, so that we can get in.'

'Sh!' said Julian, suddenly. 'I think I can hear something.' They listened, but went on again, thinking that Julian was mistaken.

But he wasn't! As they turned a dark corner that led into a cave, someone leapt at them! Julian went down to the ground at once, and Dick followed. He just had time to see that Ebenezer was there with someone else – Jacob perhaps?

As Dick fell, gold coins spilled out of his pocket. Ebenezer gave a cry and bent down to them at once. Julian tried to take his chance and slip by him – but the other man caught him and sent him spinning backwards. 'Where did you find that money? You tell us or you'll be sorry!' shouted Ebenezer, and the echo came back at once, 'Sorry – sorry – sorry!'

'Run, Dick!' panted Julian. 'It's our only chance!' He gave Ebenezer a terrific shove, which sent him into the other man – yes, it *was* Jacob, who must somehow have

escaped from police custody – and then he and Dick were off at once, running as fast as they could, back along the way they had come. 'You come here!' yelled Ebenezer, and they heard him pounding after them.

'Hurry!' panted Dick. 'If only we can get to the shaft, we're all right.'

But alas, they took the wrong turning, and soon found themselves in a cave they had never seen before. Ebenezer and Jacob blundered past without seeing them. 'Better stay here a while,' said Julian. 'Let them get a good way off.'

So they stayed still and quiet, and then at last ventured out of their hiding place and tried to find their way back to the right path.

'You know – if we get lost down here, we're done for!' said Julian. 'And once the tide flows in, we shall be in a pretty poor way! Somehow we've got to get out through the cliff way or back to the shaft. Hang on to me, Dick. We mustn't get separated, whatever happens!'

They stumbled on, not really knowing whether they were going in the right direction or not. They seemed to go through endless tunnels and caves – what a labyrinth there was in that great stratum of rocks! Then they heard voices!

'That's Ebby's voice – and Jacob's too,' whispered Julian. 'They're coming this way. Hide here, and keep still!'

So they hid quietly, and listened to Ebby and Jacob.

164

'Those boys have *got* to come back here,' said Ebby. 'We'll wait. Don't make a sound!'

'We'll have to make a dash for it, and hope for the best!' whispered Julian. 'Come on! We'll be caught by the tide soon if we're not quick!'

They both made a sudden rush, and passed the surprised Ebby and Jacob at a run. Then down the tunnel beyond them they went as fast they could, bumping their arms and legs and heads against the rocky walls, but holding their torches steadily in front of them. On they went and on – and behind them, breathing heavily, came Ebby and Jacob.

'I think this must be a bad dream!' panted Dick. 'JULIAN! JULIAN! look – there's water coming along this tunnel! The tide's coming in!'

'Come *on*,' said Julian. 'I feel as if the shaft isn't far away now. I seem to know this tunnel – and this cave. Come *on*, Dick, we haven't a minute to spare! We've GOT to get to the ladder!'

'Look! There's the shaft!' yelled Dick at last. 'Come on – we shall just about be able to squeeze under the arch at the bottom! Hurry, Julian – the water's up to our ankles now!'

They reached the shaft and squeezed under the small archway that let the water run through from side to side over the rocky bottom of the shaft. They began to mount the ladder, and then stopped to hear if there were any sounds from Ebby or Jacob.

They heard yells. 'EBBY! COME BACK! Tide's flowing in!'

and then they heard Ebby's angry voice.

'I'm coming! They've gone farther down – and they won't like it! They'll be drowned before they get much farther!'

Dick grinned. 'Come on, Ju, – up we go! I can see the light through the trap-door at the top. The girls have left it open, bless them.'

And soon the two boys were clambering out of the trap-door, with Timmy barking madly and licking their necks, the girls and Tinker too excited for words!

'What happened? Didn't you get out of the tunnel to find help for us? Were those men there? What *happened*?'

'Plenty!' said Julian. 'But unfortunately we didn't get past Ebby and Jacob, who were lying in wait for us. So we're *still* stuck in this lighthouse, with nobody to help us. BUT . . .'

'But what?' asked George, shaking his arm. 'Julian, you look excited. What's happened?'

'We found the treasure!' said Julian. 'Come on – we'll tell you all about it!' And he led the way up the spiral stairway, with Tinker and the excited girls close behind.

Soon the boys were telling their story, and George and Anne and Tinker listened and exclaimed and danced about, and were altogether marvellous listeners to a marvellous tale.

'It MUST have been the treasure – in an iron-bound chest – oh, Ju, weren't you excited when the coins poured out?'

'Yes. It was certainly a very fine moment,' said Julian.

'Mischief, stop pulling my hair. Wow! It's been an exciting morning! What about a drink of lemonade – and by the way, what's the weather been like? We couldn't see a thing down below!'

'Oh, it's *awful* again, Julian!' said Anne. 'There's another storm coming – look at those scurrying black clouds.'

'It does look bad,' said Julian, his excitement leaving him, as he saw clearly that another big storm was blowing up. 'We certainly shouldn't be able to get out of here today, even if we could get out of the door!'

'Julian, Tinker found his father's old pocket radio in a cupboard,' said Anne. 'And it still works. We listened to the weather report, and it gave an important warning to all ships at sea or by the coast. It said they must run to safety as soon as they could.'

'Well, I'm blessed if I know what to do for the best,' said Julian, looking out of the window. 'How in the world are we to let people know we're here, marooned in the light-house? We'll simply *have* to think of something!'

But that was easier said than done! How did one get help when there was no way to get help? How did one escape out of a locked lighthouse when there was no key?

CHAPTER TWENTY-ONE

A wonderful idea

'I'M THIRSTY,' said Tinker. 'I'll get some lemonade.'

'Well, go slow with it, then,' said Dick. 'You don't know how long we may be locked up here – and we haven't endless food and drink!'

Tinker looked alarmed. 'Might we be locked up here for weeks and weeks?' he said.

'If people thought we had left the lighthouse and gone back home because of the bad weather, we might easily be here for some time,' said Julian, soberly. 'Nobody would bother about us – they'd think we were safe at home.'

'But Mother would soon feel worried if she didn't hear from us,' said George. 'We said we'd send her a card each day, you know – and if she doesn't have one for a day or two, she would be sure to get worried, and send someone over here.'

'Hurrah for mothers!' said Dick, relieved. 'All the same – I don't fancy a week or so here with hardly anything to eat. We'll have plenty of one thing though – and that's rainwater!'

'There must be *some* way out of this,' said Julian who had been sitting silent, frowning at his thoughts. 'Can't we get a message out *somehow*? Are there any flags here, Tinker, that we could wave out of the window?'

'No,' said Tinker. 'I've never seen any. What about a white tablecloth? We've one of those.'

'Yes. That would do,' said Julian. 'Fetch it, Tinker.'

Tinker pulled it off the table and gave it to Julian. Julian went to the window and looked through the glass, which was misted with spray. 'I don't expect anyone will notice a tablecloth being shaken out of this window,' he said. 'But I'll try it. My word – the window's hard to open. It seems to have stuck.'

He opened it at last, and immediately an enormous gust of wind came in, and everything went flying – papers, books, carpets – chairs fell over, and poor Mischief was blown from one side of the lighthouse room to the other. Timmy barked in fright and tried to catch the flying papers as they went by his nose. The tablecloth disappeared at once!

Julian managed to close the window again after a terrific effort, and once more the room became peaceful. 'Whew!' said Julian. 'I didn't guess there was such a gale outside. I should think that tablecloth is about five miles away by now! The gulls will get a surprise when it comes flapping along in the sky.'

George couldn't help laughing at that, frightened though she was. 'Oh, Julian – it was a jolly good thing you didn't fly off with the tablecloth! My WORD, what a gale! I wonder the lighthouse stands it.'

'Well, we do feel a buffet now and again,' said Dick. 'There – did you feel that? It was either a wave bumping into the rocks or spray forced against us – I distinctly felt the lighthouse shake a little.'

'Rubbish!' said Julian, seeing Anne's scared face. 'Don't make silly jokes like that.'

'You're quite *sure* that the lighthouse can't be blown down?' said Anne, in a small voice.

'Dear Anne, use your commonsense,' said Julian. 'Would it have stood for all these years if it hadn't been strong enough to stand against storms far worse than this?'

'Mischief is feeling frightened too,' said Tinker. 'He's gone and hidden, look.'

'Well, long may he stay there,' said Julian. 'At least, he's not trying to open the biscuit tin, or delve into the bag of sweets! I should just like to know how many of our sweets he has eaten up to now!'

WHOOOOOOOOOSH!

That was an extra big gale of wind that buffeted the lighthouse, and made Timmy stand up and growl. Rain pattered against the window, sounding as if someone was throwing pebbles.

Julian was very worried. It really did look as if the stormy weather was going on and on. It might quite well continue for a few days, and their food certainly would not last long. There were still some tins left, and they had plenty of water, of course – the rain saw to that – but somehow they were all always so *hungry*!

'Cheer up, Julian,' said George. 'You do look grim.'

'I feel it,' said Julian. 'I cannot for the life of me think of any way to escape from here, or even to get help. We've no way of signalling . . .'

'Pity the lighthouse lamp is no longer going,' said

172

A WONDERFUL IDEA

Tinker. 'That would have been a fine signal.'

To Tinker's enormous surprise Julian suddenly gave a shout, leapt up, came over to Tinker, and gave him such a clap on the back that the surprised boy almost fell off his chair!

'W-w-what's the matter?' stammered Tinker, rubbing his shoulder.

'Don't you *see* – perhaps we can set the old lamp going, and make it shine out as it used to do – not to warn ships, of course – but to make people realise that we are prisoners in the lighthouse!' said Julian, jubilantly. 'Tinker – do you know if it's *possible* to light the lamp?'

'I think so,' said Tinker. 'My father showed me how it worked, and I think I remember. Oh – and there's a bell that can be struck, too!'

'Better and better!' said Julian. 'Where is the bell?'

'It was dismantled and put away,' said Tinker. 'It used to hang in that sort of verandah place that runs outside, round the lamp-room – there's a big hook for it there.'

'Oh – it hung in that outside gallery, did it?' said Julian. 'Well – that means that one of us would have to go out there in the wind and hang it up – not too good! There must be a ninety-mile-an-hour gale up there. Anyway, let's get the bell and have a look at it.'

The great bell was down in the storeroom, covered up. It was made of brass, and once had had a hammer that struck it at intervals, worked by some simple machinery. But the machinery was in pieces – no good at all!

'We'll take the bell upstairs,' said Julian. 'Gosh, it's heavy as lead. Dick, I'll want your help.'

Between them the two boys carried the heavy bell up to the living room, and Tinker brought up the old hammer that used to strike it. Julian and Dick held up the bell by its loop of iron. 'Hit it with the hammer, Tinker,' said Julian. 'See if it still sounds loudly.'

Tinker struck it hard with the hammer – and at once a great deep clang filled the room from side to side, making Timmy jump almost out of his skin. He and Mischief left the room at top speed and fell down the spiral stairway together. All the others jumped too, and stared at one another in awe. The sound of the bell went booming round and round the room, filling their ears so that they had to shake their heads to try and get rid of the sound. Julian at last clasped the rim of the bell with both his hands and the sound died away.

'What a WONDERFUL bell!' he said, in awe. 'Look how old it is, too – see, it says, "Cast in 1896"! If only we could get it hung up in its place on the gallery, the sound of it would go right to the village and beyond! I wonder how many ships heard it in the old days, booming out every now and again as the hammer struck it.'

Tinker raised the hammer again, but Dick stopped him. 'No – you saw how scared Timmy and Mischief were. They'll probably jump through a window, glass and all, if we sound the bell again!'

'We'll wait till we think the wind has died down a bit, and then try to hang the bell,' said Julian. 'Now let's look at the lamp. Will it want oil, Tinker?'

'It may do – though I think there's some still in it, left when the lighthouse was closed down,' said Tinker. 'But there is plenty down in the storeroom.'

'Good,' said Julian, feeling decidedly more cheerful. 'Now – if the gale dies down at all, we'll try to hang the bell. We can strike that as soon as it's hung, and not wait till we light the lamp.'

But the gale seemed to get worse, and Julian really did wonder if the old lighthouse would stand up to it! Should he take everyone down to the storeroom? Just in case? I will if the gale gets worse, he thought. 'Though if the lighthouse should fall, there wouldn't be much chance for us, whatever part of it we're in!'

They went up to the lamp-room in the afternoon and looked at the great old lamp. Tinker explained how it worked. 'It used to go round and round mechanically,' he said, 'and there were screens here – and here – that shut out the light in places as it went round – so that the light seemed to go on and off, if any ship was watching it – it seemed to *flash*, you see, instead of to shine steadily. Ships noticed it more quickly then.'

The screens were broken in pieces. There was still some oil in the lamp, but Julian added more. The wick seemed perfectly good. Now, if only they could light the lamp, and keep it going, someone would be sure to see it, and wonder about it!

Julian felt in his pocket for matches. As the lamp-room was enclosed in glass, it was easy to keep the match alight. He touched the oily wick with it – and, hey-presto, the lamp was lit!

It was a very big lamp, and, close to, the light was quite blinding. Dick crowed with delight. 'We've done it! Old lighthouse, you're going to shine once more tonight! You're alive again!'

'Now to hang the bell,' said Julian, and he cautiously opened the door leading on to the gallery outside, having waited until the wind died down for a moment. He and Dick lifted the bell up to the hook there and slipped the iron loop over it. It hung there, swinging, and Julian lifted

the hammer – but at that moment a great gust took him and he staggered, almost falling over the railing!

Dick caught him just in time, and, with George's help, dragged him into the lamp-room. They were all very white-faced! 'That was a narrow escape,' said George, her hands shaking and her body trembling. 'We'll have to be careful if we go out on the gallery again! Perhaps we had better rely only on the lamp.'

'I vote we all go down and have some hot tea,' said Julian, thankful for his escape. His legs felt shaky as he went down the stairs. He was not surprised! Julian was seldom scared, and it was peculiar to have legs that suddenly gave at the knees!

However, everyone soon recovered when they were drinking hot tea and eating ginger biscuits. 'I wish it was dark so that we could see how bright the light is from the lamp when it shines,' said Dick. 'It will be dark very quickly today.'

It was! So dark that the light streaming from the old lamp at the top of the lighthouse was brilliant! It cut a shining path through the night, gleaming yellow.

And through the roar of the sea went a great clanging, as Julian, with Dick holding on to him, struck the old bell hanging in the gallery.

'Listen!' said George, her hand on Timmy's collar. 'Listen! BOOM! BOO-OOO-OOM! BOOOOM! Tim, that bell must feel happy tonight – it's found its voice again!'

BOOOOOOOOOM! Has anyone heard that old bell on this stormy night? Has anyone seen the light from the old, old lamp?

BOOOOOOOOOM!!!

CHAPTER TWENTY-TWO

The end of the adventure

DOWN IN the village of Demon's Rocks that night, people
drew their curtains, made up their fires, and sat down in
their armchairs. They were thankful not to be out in the
wind and the rain.

Old Jeremiah Boogle was lighting his pipe, sitting by his
own roaring fire, when he heard a sound that made him
drop the flaring match, and listen in amazement.

BOOOOOOM! BOOOOOOM!

'A bell! A bell I've not heard for nearly forty years!' said
old Jeremiah, standing up, hardly able to believe his ears.
'No – it *can't* be the lighthouse bell. That's been gone for
many a day!'

BOOOOOOM!

Jeremiah went to his window and pulled aside the old
curtain. He stared out – and could not believe his eyes! He
gave a yell. 'MILLIE! Where's that grand-daughter of mine?
MILLIE!'

'What is it, Grandad, now?' said a plump little woman,
bustling in.

'Look, Millie – am I seeing right – isn't that the lighthouse lamp shining there?' said Jeremiah.

'Well – there's a bright light shining out there high

179

above Demon's Rocks,' said Millie. 'But I never in *my* life saw the lighthouse lamp shining out before! And what's that booming noise, Grandfather – like a wonderful great bell?'

'That's the old bell in the lighthouse!' said Jeremiah. 'I couldn't mistake that! Many's the time I heard it booming out to warn ships off Demon's Rocks in the old days. Millie, it can't be! It doesn't hang there any more. And the light doesn't shine any more. What's happening?'

'I don't know, Grandad,' said Millie, scared. 'There isn't anyone in the lighthouse, far as *I* know!'

Old Jeremiah smacked his hand down on the window-sill, knocking over a plant pot. '*There are* folk there – three boys and two girls, and a monkey too – and a dog as well!'

'Well, there now!' said Millie. 'And what would they be there for? Did *they* set the lamp going and sound that bell? BOOOOM – there it goes again – enough to wake all the babies in Demon's Rocks village!'

Millie was right. It did wake all the babies, and the children – and amazed every man and woman in the place, including Ebenezer and Jacob. They had leapt to their feet when they had heard the bell, and were astounded to see the great light shining out steadily in the night.

They heard people hurrying by their cottage, on their way to Demon's Rocks jetty. They heard Jeremiah's big voice booming out too. 'It's those children up there in the lighthouse, banging that bell, and setting that light shining. Something's wrong! It's help they're needing, folks! Something's wrong!'

Ebenezer and Jacob knew quite well what was wrong! The children were locked in the lighthouse and couldn't get out! They might be ill or hurt – or starving – but they couldn't get out to fetch help. And now the whole village was aroused, and when the morning came, a boat would bob out on the great waves and find out what had happened!

Ebby and Jacob disappeared that night! It wasn't Constable Sharp they feared – it was the people of the village! They slipped away in the dark and the rain, and were gone. But you'll be caught, Ebby, you'll be caught, Jacob! And no one will be sorry for you. No one at all!

When daylight came, there were many people on the jetty, ready to go across to the lighthouse. The wind was so rough that great waves still rolled over the rocks on which the lighthouse stood. Soon a boat was launched, and Jeremiah, Constable Sharp and the village doctor went across, the boat careering from side to side like a mad thing, as the waves caught it.

They went up the steps to the lighthouse and banged at the door – and from the other side came Julian's glad voice, 'You'll have to break down the door. Ebby and Jacob locked us in and took the key. We can't get out, and we're running short of food!'

'Right. Stand back,' shouted Jeremiah. 'Constable and I are going to break in!'

THE END OF THE ADVENTURE

Jeremiah was old but he was still hefty, and Constable Sharp was heftier still. The lock suddenly splintered under their enormous shoves, and the door flew wide open! Jeremiah and the policeman shot inside and bumped into Julian and the rest, sending them flying. Timmy barked in astonishment and Mischief fled up the stairway!

Soon they were all in the living room, and Julian was pouring out his story. Anne made tea and handed round steaming cups. Jeremiah listened open-mouthed, and the policeman busily took notes. The doctor, glad that no one was ill or hurt, sipped his tea and listened, too.

'We didn't know *how* to get out when we were locked in,' said Julian, coming to the end of his long story. 'So in the end we lit the old lamp, and hung up the old bell, and struck it with the hammer. I could hardly stand in the gallery, though, there was such a wind! I struck it for half an hour, and then my brother here went on till he felt too cold. The lamp didn't burn all night – it went out early this morning.'

'But both bell and light did their job well, son,' said Jeremiah, looking twenty years younger, he was so excited. 'Ah, to think that old lamp shone again, and that old bell sounded – I thought I must be dreaming!'

'We'll be after that Ebenezer and Jacob,' said the policeman, shutting his notebook. 'And it seems to me you'd all better go home. This weather's going on for a bit – and there's nothing to keep you here, is there?'

'Well,' said Julian, 'actually there *is* something to keep us here. You know the old wreckers' lost treasure you told us about, Jeremiah? Well – we've found it!'

Jeremiah was so astounded that he couldn't say a word! He goggled at Julian, and opened and shut his mouth like a fish. Julian took some golden coins out of his pocket and showed them to the policeman and the doctor, and to Jeremiah.

'There you are!' he said. 'We know where there are thousands of these – they are in iron-bound boxes and chests down in one of the tunnels in the rock. What do you think of that? We can't leave here till we've given the treasure into the hands of the police! It belongs to the Crown, doesn't it?'

'Yes, it does,' said Constable Sharp, gazing at the bright gold coins. 'But you'll get a fine reward – all of you will! Where's this treasure? I'd better get it straightaway.'

'Well – you have to go down the foundation shaft of the lighthouse,' said Julian, gravely, but with a twinkle in his eye, 'and crawl under the archway at the bottom, and then make your way down the tunnel – but be careful the sea doesn't catch you – and then when you come to . . .'

The policeman stopped scribbling down what Julian was saying, and looked startled. Julian laughed.

'It's all right – Dick and I will fetch it ourselves today, and give it to you, complete with every single gold coin,' he said. 'We don't *need* to go down the shaft – there's another way in – the way *you* took us, Jeremiah. We'll go this morning, for a last excitement. And then – home! Perhaps you would kindly telephone Kirrin Garage for a car to fetch us at twelve o'clock, Constable?'

'Oh *good*!' said Anne. 'An adventure is always exciting but I've really had enough at the moment! This was such a bad-weather one! Oh, Constable, look out – that monkey has pulled out your whistle!'

So he had – and what is more he blew it – PHEEEEEEEEEE! Jeremiah almost jumped out of his skin, and Mischief received a slap that almost made *him* jump out of his skin too!

'Goodbye, Jeremiah,' said Julian. 'It's been fine meeting you – and thanks for coming to rescue us. We'll see you again some day. Come along, Constable – we'll go and find the treasure with you now.'

'I don't think I'll come,' said Anne, who really didn't like dark, smelly tunnels and caves. 'I'll do the packing.'

'Timmy and I will help you,' said George, who knew that Anne wouldn't like to be left alone in the lighthouse.

The boys went off with Jeremiah, the doctor and Constable Sharp, rowing over the rocks to the jetty. The doctor and Jeremiah said goodbye at the jetty, and the three boys and Mischief took Constable Sharp to find the treasure. They had to push their way through quite a crowd of people who had collected on the quay, anxious to know why the light had shone out from the lighthouse in the night, and why the bell had sounded.

'Make way, please,' said the policeman, politely. 'Everything is all right. These children were locked in the lighthouse and couldn't get out. Make way, please.

There is no need for any excitement!'

'No – that's all over now – isn't it, Ju?' said Dick. 'Whew – it was just a bit *too* exciting at times! I shall be quite glad to be at Kirrin Cottage again, with peace and quiet all around us.'

'You've forgotten that Uncle Quentin and his friend will still be there,' said Julian, with a grin. 'There'll be plenty going on while they're around! I'm afraid they won't be at all pleased to see us back!'

Oh yes, they will, Julian – especially when they hear the exciting story you have to tell! You'll have some fun showing round a gold coin or two. Timmy is to have one hung on his collar, as a reward for guarding you so well – how proud he will be!

Well, goodbye to you all! Goodbye, Julian and Dick, and a good journey home! Goodbye, Anne and George – and Tinker too, and Mischief, you funny little monkey!

And goodbye, dear old Timmy, best of friends. How we wish we had a dog like you! See you all again some day!